+ + +

IT IS JANUARY 1885 AND LARS AND KATJA NEUFELD, brother and sister, make a daring escape from Khartoum just before the Mahdi's Muslim army capture it and slaughter the Europeans and other infidels. Disguised as Arabs, the pair follows their father's detailed plan: they sail south in a twenty-foot ketch up the Blue Nile. Their goal is to find refuge in Abyssinia, a Christian nation, migrate to German Equatoria, and then sail to Bavaria, their father's home. Their perilous adventures en route include Mahdi's soldiers, raging waters, vicious creatures, and enslavement near the Abyssinian border.

KHARTOUM

Inquiries should be addressed to the Publisher
Lamplight Press
PO Box 82516,
Austin, Texas 78708

ISBN: 978-0-9892861-8-3

Printed in the United States of America

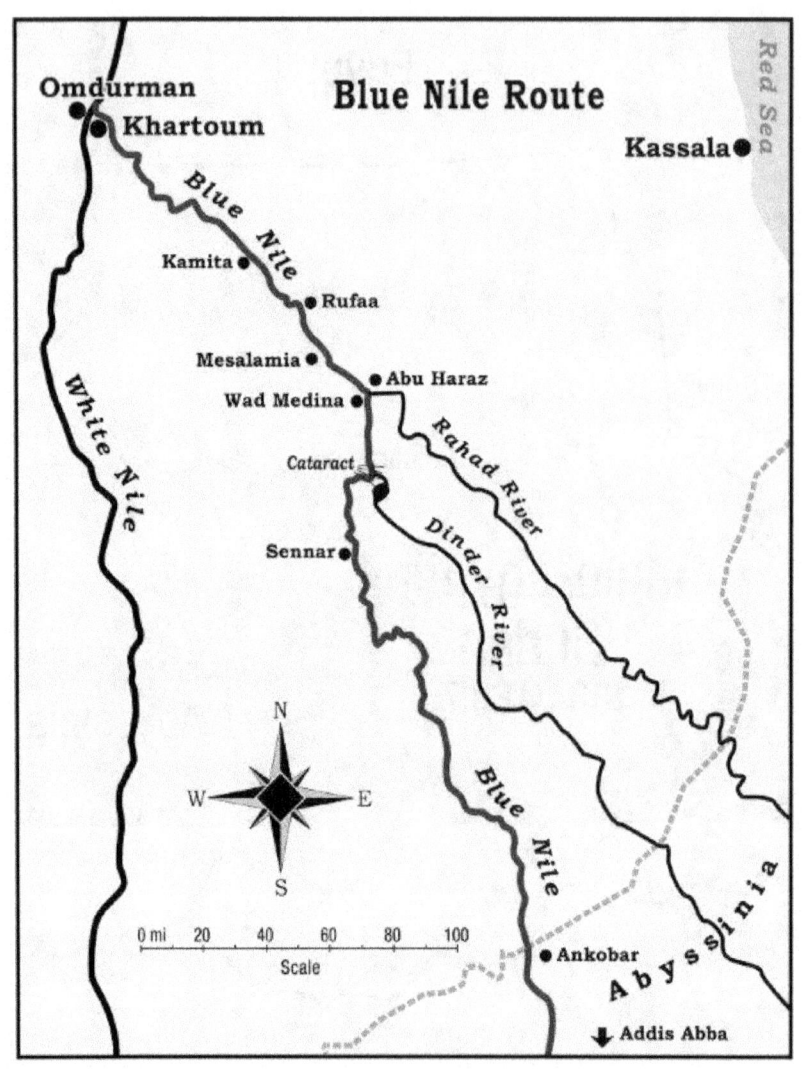

Night was falling as Dieter Neufeld quickly made his way through the deserted streets of Khartoum. "Damned perfidious British fools! They're leaving us all to be massacred by those fanatical Muslims," he muttered to himself. The unusual quiet unnerved him. Khartoum at dusk was normally bustling as residents emerged from their homes into the cooling evening, but these days they remained hidden behind heavy doors, daring only to take the evening air in the courtyards of their heavily barricaded houses. "They encouraged us to settle here, and now they play politics in London and Cairo and have abandoned us." Neufeld had just left a meeting of the city's European residents with the recently arrived British Governor General of the Anglo-Egyptian Sudan, General Charles George "Chinese" Gordon.

For nearly three years, a violent rebellion of Sudan's Arab population, fomented by a Muslim mystic, Muhammad Ahmad bin Abi Allah, had wracked the country. A few years earlier, in 1881, Ahmad had proclaimed himself the promised Mahdi, The Redeemer of all Islam, and had rallied the Sudanese tribes to his flag. His goal was to rid the Sudan of its hated Egyptian overlords and the infidel British occupiers, to establish a pure Muslim caliphate, and to impose his own radical version of Islam on the country. Through his fiery, hate-filled sermons, his religious and nationalistic ideas spread like wildfire through the Muslim population. He was now leading an ever-growing army of followers in a holy war against the hated Anglo-Egyptian government of the Sudan. He vowed to conquer Egypt, Central Africa, and Jerusalem. In a flight of fancy, he proclaimed that he would conquer the entire world and convert all infidels to the true religion.

The British government so far had displayed little initiative in defending their holdings in this part of Africa. Now, in January of 1884, the Mahdi's army had captured Omdurman, which lay just across the Nile from Khartoum, and he was tightening a noose around the Anglo-Egyptian city. After a single boat carrying some of the city's European residents to safety in Cairo had departed down the Nile, the Mahdi's armies had closed the river and Khartoum's remaining Europeans were trapped. Gordon had insufficient British and Egyptian troops to launch a full-scale assault on the Mahdi's army or even to provide an adequate defense of the coming assault on Khartoum. General Gordon could only answer the residents' demands for protection with feeble promises that British forces would be coming soon to lift the siege. No fools, Neufeld and most of the residents knew the truth—Khartoum would fall to the Mahdi.

Khartoum was the capital city of the Sudan. Its strategic location at the apex of the triangle formed by the confluence of the White and Blue Nile Rivers controlled access to central Africa. It was the seat of the British colonial government and an important commercial transshipment center. It was also the linchpin in Great Britain's long-term goal of hegemony athwart central Africa from the Mediterranean to the Cape of Good Hope. Khartoum was a mid-sized, dusty squalor of mud brick huts, twisting dirt streets, and dark alleys. Its population was about thirty-four thousand souls--mostly Arabs. The Europeans who inhabited the city worked for the Anglo-Egyptian government, were engaged in commerce, or ran the Western schools and hospital. There were a few multi-story buildings, a number of European-style shops in the commercial center, and villas surrounded by shaded gardens in the European residential quarter. Numerous Muslim minarets dotted the skyline. Government and commercial buildings were concentrated in the apex of the two rivers and in the area that bordered the White Nile. To the south along the White Nile were a small-boat harbor and the commercial dock area with six industrial piers. Inland a few hundred feet were a number of large commercial warehouses and the military barracks. By most measures, Khartoum was a thriving, important colonial center. But the revolutionary chaos in the surrounding desert and occasional loud gatherings of the Mahdi's supporters in the city's main streets had placed a heavy pall of fear and suspense over the city.

Neufeld moved purposefully through the quiet streets, which were lit only by the vast panorama of desert stars in the black sky. His energy was driven by his impatience with General Gordon's dissembling and the perfidy of the British government, and by fear for the fate of his family, and he knew how deeply the Sudanese hated their Egyptian overlords and the Europeans who were reaping the riches of these desert lands. He also understood the volatile nature of the local Arabs and how easily they were seduced by the Mahdi, who was not only an inspiring leader but offered them a messianic vision of a new age governed by Islamic law.

"Khartoum is doomed!" he said to himself as he made his way down the street toward his home. Neufeld was a tall man with broad shoulders and graying hair, but thin to the point of gauntness. Several times during his short walk from the Governor's Palace, he was overcome by an attack of violent coughing that left him breathless and hunched against a wall. "Damn pipe," he gasped. "I must stop smoking."

Neufeld knew for certain, despite General Gordon's assurances, that there would be no help from the British army. The inhabitants of Khartoum had been abandoned by the British government, and the British garrison billeted in the city was too small and too poorly armed to defend it long against the Mahdi's army. The meeting had adjourned as the Europeans erupted in panic and outrage. Neufeld reckoned that soon Khartoum would fall to the Mahdi, and that escape for the besieged Western residents would be impossible.

However, for several months Neufeld has been devising a plan to save his two children--all that remained of his family. When he had been denied a place for them on the refugees' boat to Cairo—priority having been given to colonial personnel and their families, and to wealthy locals whose well-being was deemed critical by the British government—he had experienced several days of sickening helplessness, knowing the horror that lay ahead for all the Europeans who remained. Then he accepted the cruel reality that the Neufelds were on their own and he began to devise a desperate plan to save them.

Dieter Neufeld had always prided himself on his resourcefulness, and he felt confident that this quality, combined with the methodical Germanic attention he gave to every detail of life, would offer his children their best chance of survival in the midst of the violent upheavals around them. His mind turned over and over again the components of his plan, flinching away whenever it came upon the possibility of failure. It could not fail, he reminded himself. For his children to remain in Khartoum meant ruthless slavery and certain death. Escape was their only hope, however fragile and precarious it was.

Neufeld had lived in Africa since he was a young man when his family emigrated from Bavaria. At first, they lived in Cairo and established a fashionable jewelry shop. When his mother contracted consumption, his father took her back to Germany. Dieter continued to manage the shop and married the beautiful Frieda—the daughter of the German ambassador. After the British occupied the Sudan, he moved his shop to Khartoum to have closer access to central Africa and its bountiful treasures. A skilled goldsmith and an expert in the cutting and mounting of precious gems, Neufeld found an eager market for his creations among the more prosperous local Arabs and British settlers in the city. Several years later, when his business had grown to the point that he had developed an international clientele, he needed help. Fortunately, his client, the Grand Khalifa of Khartoum, Ishan al-Numan, suggested that Neufeld consider hiring his young niece Rahmah to deal with his Arab clients.

That afternoon Rahmah was working the counter. She was efficient, pleasant, and quickly became knowledgeable about his inventory and the scope of the jewelry business. While at work, she did not wear the traditional abaya and niqab. Instead, she wore a loose-fitting Western dress and a scarf over her hair. She had no fear that the imams would cause her trouble because of her European dress. Her uncle had given her permission to wear a Western costume as a courtesy to his favorite jeweler. Neufeld's clients often remarked how pleased they were with Rahmah's courtesy and professionalism. Dieter Neufeld and his wife, Frieda, treated her as if she were part of their still-childless family.

One morning Rahmah stumbled into Neufeld's shop. She was crying, her face bruised and flushed, and her hair uncovered and disheveled. The left side of her dress was soaked in blood. She gasped through her sobs, "Rape! I've been raped! My uncle, Ihsan the holy man, raped me. He attacked me in my own home while my father was at work." Neufeld helped her to his chair and summoned his wife.

Frieda calmed Rahmah and took her upstairs into the Neufelds' apartment. After a warm bath, lotions, and hot tea, Rahmah submitted to Frieda's inspection. "No serious physical harm, my dear Rahmah. You should be completely healed in a week or so."

"Ihsan deflowered me. Now I am unclean. My family will disown me. No man will ever marry me." Rahmah began to sob uncontrollably.

Rahmah and the Neufelds knew the uselessness and danger of complaining to the local imam about her rape because the stringent rules of Sharia law required the testimony of four male witnesses for prosecuting a rapist. And because Rahmah's uncle was a senior cleric, such a complaint would be particularly perilous. Frieda took Rahmah in her arms and tried to console her. "We'll look after you, Rahmah. You're part of our family. Stay with us. We'll notify your father that you're living with us for a while. We can tell him that we're working late hours because of the comprehensive inventory we're taking, and that we don't feel you'd be safe walking home late at night. I'm sure he'll agree."

Rahmah fell back on the bed and closed her tear-reddened eyes. After a few moments she said, "I am now an outcast in my own society. You offer me the only option I have. I thank you with all my heart, and I shall love you like my own deceased mother."

A few months later, it was obvious that Rahmah was pregnant. The Neufelds could hide her condition for only so long. Then Rahmah had to remain upstairs in the apartment out of sight. Dieter Neufeld told Rahmah's father and any clients who asked about her that she was ill with a fever, and that Frieda is taking care of her in their spare bedroom.

One evening, shortly after delivering a healthy boy, Rahmah carried her child into the Neufelds' parlor, where Dieter and Frieda sat reading. Dieter could see that the young woman's face was stained with tears, and her voice was choked with misery. After a moment of hesitation, she spoke softly. "With the deepest sorrow, I beg you to adopt my baby and baptize him in your Christian religion. I love him so much, but I cannot be an unmarried mother in this Muslim country, nor can my son be the bastard offspring of a whore, which is how people would regard me if they knew what had happened to me." With more tears forming, she whispered, "If the secret of my child's birth ever becomes known, the imams will issue a fatwa and rally the faithful to stone me to death as an adulteress." She kissed her newborn tenderly, then handed him to Frieda.

With Christian charity, the Neufelds agreed to her request. Frieda embraced Rahmah and kissed her, and tears rolled down both their cheeks. "Of course we'll adopt your child, my dear Rahmah. We'll love and raise him as our own son, and we'll teach him to be an honorable man."

Dieter stood and took the baby from his wife. He looked for a moment into the infant's face, then turned to Rahmah. "We understand your plight, my dear, and we'll do our best to protect your son, and you as well. You will always have a home with us, and you'll be able to help us raise this fine boy."

Frieda consulted with Dieter, and then she looked at Rahmah and said, "With your permission, we'll name our new son Lars. This was the name of Dieter's father, and in your boy the name will continue to live with honor."

A few mornings later, Rahmah did not appear for breakfast, and Frieda saw that her bed had not been disturbed. On inspection, she realized that Rahmah had decamped during the night, without leaving a note. Dieter speculated, "She has probably gone to visit her father. She'll return in a few days." But the Neufelds never saw Rahmah again.

Several days later, Neufeld was reading the lead article in Khartoum's English newspaper, The Nile News. It said, "The Grand Khalifa of Khartoum, Ihsan al-Numan, was found murdered in his study with multiple stab wounds. The autopsy revealed that the victim had been castrated. Chief Inspector Nigel Featherstone-Hough, CBE, is working with Muslim clerics to solve this sacrilegious murder. The Inspector reported that there are no clues, and inquiries are continuing." Neufeld placed the newspaper on his desk, picked up his calabash pipe, carefully filled it with his favorite tobacco, struck a match, and lit the tobacco. He leaned back in his chair and drew deeply, savoring the excellent flavor of the well-cured Latakia. As he slowly exhaled and the smoke drifted upward, he wondered what had become of Rahmah.

Eighteen months later, the Neufelds were delightfully surprised when Frieda conceived. At the appropriate time, Frieda delivered a beautiful baby girl during a difficult breech birth. Unfortunately, the doctor could not stop Frieda's bleeding, and she expired the next day. Heartbroken, Neufeld named the baby girl Katja, his deceased mother's name, and vowed to raise his children with all the love and care he had. He hired an Arab wet nurse for the baby and the widow of a fallen Welsh infantryman as a nanny to help with the children and maintain the apartment.

Neufeld raised Lars in the Lutheran faith, and the boy graduated with high honors from St. Paul's School, focusing his studies on business and economics. Because of the school's emphasis on Christian theology and the display of the cross, it was located within the Governor's palace grounds. Lars was a handsome fellow, slightly over six feet tall, with broad shoulders, long muscular arms, and the olive complexion of the local Sudanese. His alert countenance glowed with shrewd black eyes, thin lips, a square jaw, and jet-black hair. He was gentle, sensitive, and brilliant, fluent in German, English, French, and Arabic. Neufeld had been training him to take over the business, and Lars was their clients' primary contact. He knew from early childhood of his birth mother's plight and the circumstances of her disappearance. He loved Neufeld as if he were his blood father and was the staunch protector of his adored sister, Katja.

At eighteen, Katja was a tall, beautiful young woman with long black hair, large dark eyes set well apart under a rosy brow, high cheekbones, a large mouth sensitively carved, and a classic Victorian hourglass figure. She was intelligent beyond her years, adroit, resourceful, and strong-willed. She had been an outstanding student at the École Française des Jeunes Filles, although her rambunctious energy and tomboyish ways had occasionally earned her the displeasure of the genteel nuns who ran the school. She also was fluent in several languages, and since finishing her education worked in their shop and managed their small household.

The Neufeld family often enjoyed their Sundays sailing the White and Blue Nile rivers in their stout twenty-foot sloop with a large mainsail and jib. Lars and Katja had become accomplished sailors when they were still children, and Katja, freed on the river from the strictures of Victorian ladyhood, relished the excitement and physical challenge of sailing. One Sunday, while sailing near the west bank of the Blue Nile, a large crocodile, about eighteen feet long, slipped out of a mass of thick papyrus reeds that concealed a small cove. The reptile swam parallel to the sloop for some distance. Neufeld cautioned his children, "Remain still. The beast will leave when he realizes that our sloop will not make a decent meal." After a few minutes, the reptile slipped away.

To relieve the tension, Katja quipped, "Obviously, that reptile does not fancy German flesh."

As military tensions built, Neufeld quietly began to implement an escape plan for his children. He purchased two Webley-455 revolvers and two Martini Henry Mark I rifles. While it was still possible to leave the city safely, he took Lars and Katya frequently into the desert south of Khartoum for target practice. Both children had been taught to handle guns when they were still very small, their father being convinced that it was the responsibility of every European resident in the colonies to be able to protect themselves. As a child, Katja was a reluctant student, preferring to ride her horse at breakneck speeds across the sands, but now she understood her father's goal--that she and Lars must have the will and means to defend themselves in the chaos building in the Sudan. In a few weeks under Neufeld's careful guidance, Lars and Katja became expert marksmen with their new weapons.

After the Madhi's army captured Omdurman, General Gordon and all those with reason understood that very soon the Mahdi would tighten the siege to Khartoum. Gordon's force of a few hundred British troops and seven thousand poorly-led, badly-trained, and ill-equipped Egyptian and loyal Sudanese black soldiers was incapable of thwarting the Madhi's army of fifty thousand frenzied Arab and African warriors. The General's repeated requests for British army reinforcements were deferred as Prime Minister Gladstone and the British Parliament equivocated about Britain's responsibility for the Sudan.

Neufeld reasoned that without massive reinforcements Khartoum would fall to the Mahdi, and that even if Parliament acted with dispatch, a force sufficient to defend Khartoum would not arrive in time to save the city. At the end of February, one Sunday evening after dinner, Neufeld decided to share with his children his conviction that eventually the Madhi's Muslim army would overwhelm the city. He knew there was little time left to complete his plans for their escape and to send them on their way to safety.

Lars countered his father's assessment of Khartoum's plight with assured conviction. "Papa, as soon as the British relief column arrives from Egypt, the Mahdi and his warriors are doomed. The Queen's regiments will conquer the Mahdi's savages with superior firepower, military tactics, and sterling British resolve. Isn't that so?"

Neufeld took Lars's hand and said in a matter-of-fact voice, "Lars, my son, you've been misled by the false optimism in the newspapers and by casual street talk. There will be no relief column. Khartoum is doomed." A spasm of coughing seized him. In a minute or so, he said, "Excuse me, I must be catching a cold." He pulled his handkerchief from his pocket and wiped his face, being careful not to let his children see the blood that he wiped from his mouth.

"Let's continue. Even if Parliament were to authorize an expedition, it could not reach us in time. To save Khartoum would take the entire British army here right now." Neufeld glanced at Katja to see if she was paying attention. Since clearing away the dishes, she had rejoined the men at the dinner table. "My dire comments reflect our perilous situation. There will be no more evacuations of civilians from Khartoum. The Nile flowing north into Egypt is closed by the Mahdi's followers. Hope for relief is foolhardy. My dear children, you need to understand and accept to the depths of your souls that I have outlined the reality of our city's grim future."

Lars took a deep breath with the intention of challenging his father. However, a slow and painful realization that his father was correct dawned across his troubled face. "Papa," he finally asked, "are you sure? No question?"

"None, Lars. None whatsoever. Facts and reason prevail."

"Then what are we to do?"

Neufeld took a deep breath and cleared his throat. His face tightened with resolve. "Let's continue. I have a plan for us." He looked sternly at his two children, who were bending toward him, their faces reflecting their troubled mixture of fear and anticipation. He could feel his heart pounding in his chest. From this moment on, he knew, there would be no turning back. The comfortable life they all knew was about to end, and what lay ahead was fraught with danger and extremely uncertain at best.

"What I want you to do is sail up the Blue Nile as far as you can, then make your way overland to Ankobar in Abyssinia. This is a Christian nation, and you will be safe there. Eventually you can make your way to German Equatoria in East Africa, and from there migrate to our family home in Bavaria."

Lars and Katya gazed at him in disbelief. Lars was the first to speak. "Papa, that's impossible! Abyssinia is hundreds of miles up the river, and Equatoria even farther. We can't possibly travel so far."

"On the contrary, my son. I have considered the details, and I believe that with initiative, courage, and some luck, it can be done." He gazed sternly at his children, the sight of their shocked faces wrenching his heart. "This is my plan. Listen carefully." They leaned toward him attentively.

"Tomorrow, Lars, you and I will paint the sloop a dull black, so it will be less visible at night. Then we'll move it to that cove in the Blue Nile where we saw the crocodile. We'll hide the boat there in the papyrus. That way no one will observe us as we prepare for your journey. We'll load the boat with supplies and everything else you'll need. On Friday night there will be no moon, so it will be less likely that you'll be seen as you make your way to the boat. By morning you'll be far up the river, away from the Mahdi's army."

"Friday!" gasped Katja. "But, Papa, that's only five days away."

Neufeld gazed at his daughter. He felt like his heart was about to break with the agony of sending his beautiful daughter off on such a desperate expedition. For a moment he clenched his jaw and lowered his eyes to the map in front of him, struggling to control the tears that he felt welling in his eyes and the anguish that wanted to choke his voice. Then he took a deep breath and turned back to her.

"This is your only chance. Now that the Mahdi has taken Omdurman, he will turn his attention to Khartoum. This city will very soon be surrounded by his army, and anyone trying to leave will be shot on sight. As each night passes, the moon will grow brighter and it will become more difficult to avoid detection. You must leave on Friday."

Stunned at the enormity of Neufeld's charge, Katja gazed at him silently for a long moment. Then she asked, "Papa, you keep talking about this escape plan as if you intend it only for Lars and me. What about you? Surely you're coming with us?"

Neufeld watched the smoke from his pipe drift upward, and after a long pause he responded, "Katja, I plan to remain here for awhile." Suppressing a cough, he continued, "I'm too old and weary and could not make such an arduous trip. I would be a hindrance to your escape and endanger you. I am counting on you, my children, to succeed."

Katja stood, put her hands on the table palms down, and countered in a voice louder than she intended, "But, Papa, how will you escape? What plan do you have? To remain in Khartoum is suicide. The Muslims will show you no mercy. You know that! You must come with us. Lars and I are both strong. We'll help you. We can all make this trip together. I know we can!"

Lars pleaded, "Papa, you're not making sense. Katja is correct. You can't remain in Khartoum. We're a family. You must leave with us."

Neufeld looked at each of his children with sympathetic eyes. He felt close to tears, overwhelmed by their love and by his own frantic fear for their future. Nearly choking with emotion, he replied, "My dear, loving children, your entreaties are compelling. But as the head of this family, I have made my own plans to evade capture, and my decision is firm. I cannot come with you to Abyssinia, and neither can you follow me on the path I have chosen. This plan is our only hope of survival. Our only hope! Be assured that the Muslims will not snag Dieter Neufeld. My German resolve will guide me." He smiled with reassurance at his children. "We shall meet again in Bavaria."

He was interrupted by another spasm of coughing that left him breathless, his brow covered with sweat. Slowly he regained control over his voice and sat forward to speak again.

"Now, to continue my plan for your escape." He unfolded a large map of the Sudan and Central Africa, spread it on the table, and with the nub of his fountain pen traced the key points of his narrative.

"Escape by steamer down the White Nile to Egypt is not an option. The Madhi's forces dominate both sides of the river for most of its course to Metuma, and their picket lines and thorn-bush zerbas have sealed the overland route south through the desert." Swinging his pen to the east, he continued, "The Madhi's warriors also control Kassala and all the other Red Sea ports." He looked at Lars, then at Katja. In his most patriarchal voice, he stated clearly and decisively, "Your only option is to leave the city by the east wall, and use our sloop to sail up the Blue Nile. A few days ago, one of our clients, an officer on General Gordon's staff, told me that the Madhi's senior emir has posted only a few pickets on the west side of the Blue Nile, and that there may be none at all on the east side. Sailing on a moonless night, with some luck, you should manage to clear the pickets. Sail close to the east shore because it is less explored and traveled. Such a route offers the best hope for a successful journey."

He looked sternly at his children to silence the protests he could see mounting within them. There was no time for cajoling or persuasion. This was their only hope, and he had to make his plans clear to them. He saw their posture change as the fierce intensity of his gaze fell on them.

Neufeld continued outlining their escape route on the maps of the Blue Nile and Central Africa. "Please understand that these maps are the best available, but they aren't totally accurate. Much of this area has not been explored or surveyed by white men." He leaned back in his chair and drew deeply on his pipe. Apprehension leaked from his eyes as he pondered the difficult and dangerous task he had assigned to Lars and Katja. He rationalized that no matter the hazards, his children's mettle would prevail. If not, almost any fate would be better than being slaughtered by the Mahdi's army or living out what remained of their lives as Muslim slaves. Katja's fate would be unthinkable.

He continued his briefing. "Be aware that you will pass two or three villages in a day or so. They are mostly small conglomerations of mud huts and are either abandoned or sparsely populated. Nonetheless, be cautious." Neufeld paused, refilled his pipe, and gazed at his children. "Am I clear?" Katja answered for both of them, "Yes, Papa." Her face was tight with sadness and fear. "Your instructions are crystal clear."

Neufeld could see how his daughter struggled for self-control, how tensely she was suppressing tears. He felt a warm surge of pride rush through his pain-wracked breast. The girl had courage, no doubt about it. She'd need it.

"Very well," he continued. Neufeld leaned close to the map and used his pen to trace a southerly course along the Blue Nile. "About one hundred seventy miles upriver is the Blue's first major tributary, the Rahad River. It is wide and flows with moderate force from the east into the Blue Nile. There are two Mahdi-controlled towns on either side of the river at this confluence. Be cautious in this area and sail through at night with your weapons at the ready. Also, Arab slavers have reported that crocodiles and venomous serpents are pervasive and aggressive south of this point. Be warned."

Lars leaned close to the map to study the details his father had described. Katja crossed her arms and shuddered slightly.

Neufeld saw that his children were paying close attention. "About twenty-five miles farther south is another tributary, the Dinder River. It rushes down from the mountains of Abyssinia through a series of long, narrow gorges and has numerous waterfalls--some over fifty feet high. Be cautious as you approach the Dinder. It is narrow, runs fast, and cascades into the Blue Nile with dramatic force." He stopped to cough again, and took a long drink of water. "Excuse me," he gasped. "All this talking, and the air is so dry." He wiped his brow, then tucked his handkerchief back in its pocket.

"From this confluence southward," he continued, tracing the line of the river with his pen, "I don't know if the Blue Nile is navigable. Nonetheless, try to broach the confluence and continue on the Blue as far as possible. At some point, however, the river will be too narrow, swift, and wild for sailing and you will have to beach the sloop on the river's west bank, retrieve your supplies, sink your boat, and travel on foot to Abysinnia. At all costs, avoid the well-developed caravan routes. They're probably controlled by the Mahdi's dervishes--the fanatical Fuzzy Wuzzies."

Lars, with a long face of concern, commented, "We understand, Papa. We'll sink the sloop, and if the opportunity presents itself, we'll purchase camels."

"Be careful, Lars. I would suggest that you try to avoid any contact with Arabs." With his most authoritative voice Neufeld commanded, "Deal only with Africans, but be careful--some of the Nubians are sympathetic to the Madhi's cause. Always have your weapons at the ready, and if you suspect treachery, fire. Leave no one alive to disclose your presence."

"We cannot be so barbaric!" cried Katja in angry disbelief as she leaped from her chair and stood with her arms akimbo. Her lips quivered in disbelief that her father would charge them to murder anyone. "It is not the Christian way. It's against all that you have taught us. Surely we can trust the blacks. They hate the Arabs for raiding their villages and enslaving the surviving inhabitants."

Neufeld focused his eyes intensely on his daughter. "My dear Katja, you must understand that some Africans support the Mahdi. Some have even joined his army." Neufeld paused and swirled his fingers over the map as he formed his next comments. He looked up and refocused on Katja. "You must do as I charge. Desperate times require desperate and unorthodox measures. You know very well what happens to Christians captured by the Mahdi's forces--especially to European women. Your primary and only responsibility is to survive. Accordingly, you must do whatever is necessary to protect your honor and your life. It is a matter of self-defense and self-preservation to keep your body inviolate."

Katja stared at her father with questioning eyes. In a few moments, she dropped her chin to her chest and her anger faded as she realized that her father's rationale superseded her objections. She closed her eyes, slumped into her chair, and nodded that she understood. She shuddered as she pictured herself in the hands of one of the Madhi's sheiks. No longer with reservations, she resolved to comply with her father's extraordinary behest. "Yes, Papa, I understand."

Neufeld picked up his pen again. "About twenty miles south of the Dinder, on the west bank of the Blue Nile, is the holy city of Senaar. If you are walking on that side of the river, travel only at night, and move inland a mile or so away from the road that follows the course of the river." He traced his pen down the Blue Nile to the Abyssinian border and pointed to Ankobar. "From Senaar, it's about a hundred and thirty miles to Abyssinia. This is a Christian nation, but you must proceed cautiously nonetheless. Dervish raiding parties frequently sortie into the border provinces in search of blacks to enslave. The Nile News recently quoted General Gordon, who reports that now that the Mahdi controls Nubia and all of the southern Sudan, the notorious slaver Pasha Zobeir Rahamma has resumed his despicable business. Gordon maintains that the British are powerless to interfere."

"Whom can we trust in this damnable war?" exclaimed Lars in disgust. Katja quickly answered, "Ourselves. Only ourselves."

"Precisely!" Neufeld commented as he returned to his escape plan, and with his pen he traced his children's course inside Abyssinia. "Work your way to Ankobar near the border. Then take the road to Addis Ababa and contact the Germany legation there for assistance in traveling on to our province Equatoria in East Africa." He paused for a moment to clear his throat. "Questions?"

Lars was the first to speak. "Papa, you've outlined a thoughtful and ambitious plan. Katja and I will succeed. Count on it."

Neufeld with narrow eyes and with his most demanding stare commanded, "You have no other option." He folded the maps and continued, "Lars, tonight we'll start to pack your survival equipment into knapsacks. I've been gathering some basic foodstuffs--canned meat and vegetables, biscuits, dry cheese, smoked sausages, and dates. In addition, I've purchased several kegs and filled them with fresh water. Yesterday, I added two extra boxes of ammunition and two trench knives in scabbards to the cache." Realizing the nearly insurmountable hazards that his children would have to endure to make a successful escape to Abyssinia, Neufeld had made another heart-rending decision. He would tell Lars about it later.

The following day, Neufeld and Lars painted the sloop and moved it from its berth in the small-boat harbor to the White Nile's confluence with the Blue Nile, then down the Blue to the crocodile cove. Later, around midnight, the two men approached Khartoum's east wall. Lars was leading their horse-drawn wagon. They had taken care to oil all the axles and hinges so they would not be betrayed by the screech of a rusty hinge. The wagon was laden with well-stuffed knapsacks and the heavy kegs of water. Not to their surprise, they saw that the Egyptian sentries had abandoned their post. In the event that these irresponsible soldiers had actually remained where they were assigned to protect the city, Neufeld had been prepared to bribe them with British pounds to let him and Lars pass unchallenged.

Proceeding as cautiously as possible, they reached the crocodile cove on the Blue Nile in about thirty minutes. No Muslim picket had challenged them, and fortunately, the reptile was not in the cove. To remain unnoticed, they worked silently, using mostly gestures to communicate and barely whispering when necessary. In a couple of hours, they had completed fitting out their sloop. Their return to the city went without incident.

As they were walking through the empty streets back to their shop, Lars commented, "Papa, our sortie to the sloop went well. Perhaps such good fortune portends success for Katja and me." Neufeld stopped and took his son's arm. Turning the boy to face him, Neufeld replied quietly but with compelling urgency, "Lars, this mission tonight was simple. Do not delude yourself about the difficulties and dangers that await you on your escape up the Blue Nile."

Neufeld continued walking toward his shop. He was silent but his face was tight with thought. This was the time he had chosen to reveal his deepest concern to his son. A couple of street-blocks later, he stopped again, faced Lars, and firmly grasped his son's arm. With his brow deeply furrowed and a fierce urgency in his voice he demanded, "Listen to me carefully, Lars. With filial loyalty, you must obey this final command I am going to give you. You must swear that you will comply with it resolutely and without hesitation."

Lars, puzzled, looked at his father. "I thought all our plans were complete. What now is so compelling that I must swear an oath to obey before I even know what you ask?"

"Because of its horrendous import, I have withheld this charge until this last moment when we are alone."

"Horrendous? I don't understand, Papa. You speak in riddles."

"Lars, we've been a loving family, and you've always trusted me to guide you. Now you must swear before I continue. Rely on our love and trust for guidance."

Convinced by his father's sound logic, Lars demurred, "Very well, Papa. I swear to do as you command."

With a catch in his authoritative voice, Neufeld continued, "Should you be in a desperate situation and capture is imminent, save a bullet for Katja."

Lars gasped at his father's charge, narrowed his eyes, and prepared to respond with questioning hostility. In a flash, however, he understood. No matter the love he had for Katja, he knew that he must not allow the Muslims to capture her. The consequences would be too gruesome to consider.

Friday arrived quickly. As the last light faded from the desert sky, Khartoum's dusty streets fell silent, unlit except for the occasional glow of a lantern or cooking fire. The new moon would not rise until just before dawn, and the city and surrounding desert lay in heavy darkness. The prevailing north breeze blew gently. The Neufeld family stood together at the east wall, well away from the guarded gate. Lars and Katja were ready to leave. Lars wore traditional Muslim garb--a worn-looking white thobe robe and the white cap worn by most Muslim men around Khartoum. He had not shaved since his father revealed their escape plan in order to look more like a local Muslim. Katja was also dressed as a man in clothes that Neufeld had purchased several weeks earlier. Her long thobe was extra large to conceal her generous femininity, but Katja had tailored the sleeves and collar to make the garment fit better. Earlier she had cut her black hair as short as a man's, and her cap was large enough to conceal some of her face. She had also rubbed brown ink into the skin of her face and hands to hide her pale European complexion. Both children wore dark, somewhat ragged abba cloaks that further concealed them. The disguises were not perfect, but Neufeld believed they would be sufficient to protect his children in the dark nights when he expected they would be traveling. Taped to their bodies were dozens of precious gems and St. George gold sovereigns. With wet eyes, they embraced their father. Lars affirmed hopefully, "Father, in a year or two, we'll be a family again and living in your fatherland. We love you dearly. God be with you."

Katja grabbed her father and held him tight. She sobbed plaintively. Through her tears she mumbled, "Papa, I cannot leave you." She placed her head on Neufeld's shoulder and squeezed him tighter. "I won't go without you, Papa. Come with us. I know we can make this trip together. Please, Papa, don't leave us." She was convulsed with anguish at the reality of leaving her father and the only family and home she had ever known, and she was acutely afraid of the perilous adventure ahead her. Yet Katja also knew the horror that awaited her if she remained in Khartoum. The dilemma wracked her soul. Though born in the Sudan, Katja was a sheltered European woman living in a brutally savage African backcountry. Her sobbing continued unabated.

Soon Neufeld unwrapped her arms from around his neck and stepped slightly away. He took her hands in his and looked at her with all the fatherly love he had. "Katja, I cannot go with you. You know that as well as I. This is a journey for the young and the strong, which I am not. I have my own plan, and I shall be fine on my own. Remember, you are a Neufeld and a German. You must have the courage of our name and our heritage." He planted a tender kiss on her brow and continued, "I have confidence that your mettle will see you safely through your journey."

Lars gently took Katja's arm. "Sister, we must go before the north wind dies."

"I know. I know," Katja whispered through her tears. "Goodbye, Papa. I love you. We'll meet again soon."

Neufeld watched his children scale the wall. They're strong, he thought, and they have courage. If anyone could survive the maelstrom of violence swirling around them, it would be Lars and Katja. He held himself proudly until they passed over the wall and vanished on the other side.

Then with shoulders drooping he walked back to his shop. Wearily, he entered the apartment, momentarily stunned by the silence and the absence of his children. "Dear God, please protect them," he whispered. "Watch over them and guide them to safety." A heavy tear rolled down his pale cheek. He was suddenly seized by a fit of coughing that shook his body nearly to collapse. When he finished, his handkerchief was sodden with blood.

He staggered across the room and located his secret stash of laudanum. Once again he whispered hoarsely, "God, protect my children. Forgive me for what I am about to do." He took a deep breath and lifted the bottle to his mouth, quickly swallowing the contents. Between coughs, he emptied the bottle. Then he lay down on the marital bed, relieved to know that he had bested the cancer eating his lungs and that the fanatical Muslims assaulting his city would not have another Christian to slaughter. The pain that had been nagging him for several months began to ease ever so slightly. He closed his eyes and dreamed of being with Frieda.

+ + +

Lars led the way up the rope ladder. At the top, he turned to look back at his father standing below them. How frail and thin the old man looked. Until this moment, Lars had not allowed himself to realize that the powerful man who had guided his life for as long as he could remember had vanished. How could he leave his beloved father now, he asked himself, now that he was so weak and obviously ill? The boy's spirit revolted at the thought. But this journey was what his father wanted of him, Lars knew. He had to be a man now, as strong and resolute as his father had always been. Lars struggled to hold back a sob and lifted his arm in a farewell salute. Turning, he clambered quickly down the other side of the wall, swallowing his tears.

Katja lingered at the top of the wall, sobbing quietly. "Hurry!" Lars whispered to her. He wanted to comfort his sister at the loss of everything she knew and loved, but this was not the time, he knew. Besides, if he allowed himself to console her, he feared that he too would burst into tears. He had to be strong. "Hurry," he whispered again.

As soon as Katja reached the ground, Lars led the way to the cove where their boat was hidden. He could hear her muffled sobs behind him but dared not stop or even acknowledge them. They had advanced about a hundred yards when a shout penetrated the darkness. "Stop! Who are you?" demanded a Muslim picket. "Come here! Let me see you."

Lars responded, "I'm escaping from the Christian infidels with my brother. Praise Allah."

"Show yourself!"

Lars replied in a soft voice, "It's so dark that I cannot see. Keep talking and I'll come to you." Lars cautioned Katja to be quiet and hide behind some nearby bushes. Drawing his knife, he advanced toward the sentry's voice. His heart was pounding, and the knife's handle felt as if it were on fire in his cold, damp hand.

In a few seconds, they stood face to face. The picket had his rifle at the ready. "What are you doing out here in the dark?" he demanded. "Up to no good, I suspect." He gestured over his shoulder. "Come with me to my watch commander."

Quickly, before the sentry could react, Lars underhanded his knife into the sentry's sternum and ripped it upward. Without a sound, the sentry fell dead.

Shaking with the enormity of having taken a man's life, Lars returned for Katja. In a low, quivering voice he whispered, "Come quickly. I've just killed the sentry. We must leave here now."

Katja gasped but managed to control any additional reactions. Wordlessly they hurried to the cove, loaded the remaining supplies into the sloop, raised the mainsail and jib, and shoved off into the Blue Nile as the north wind filled their sails. Lars felt numb from fear and grief at leaving their father, and he could see from Katja's silent, mechanical movements as they launched the boat that she was also overwhelmed with emotion.

In the pitch darkness, Lars navigated their sloop slowly and silently up the Blue Nile as the north wind held steady, filling the sails. His mind whirled with horrific thoughts and frightening emotions. Over and over, he kept dipping his hands into the river to wash away the blood of the picket he killed. Echoing incessantly in his mind was the startled death gasp of the man he had slain. He wondered if he had the mental and physical mettle to accomplish this perilous journey, and to obey his father's last charge about Katja. The effort to suppress his fear exhausted him, but Lars knew he had to remain strong and calm. Katja needed his strength, and his father was depending on him to lead them both to safety.

After several hours, he reckoned that they had passed the last of the Muslim pickets. Sunrise was near, and Lars guided the sloop into a small inlet on the east bank and Katja dropped the anchor into the dark water. The black sky began to grow lighter, and then suddenly they were surrounded by the glare of the rising sun.

In the harsh light, Katja looked haggard, her eyes red and swollen from crying, her cheeks stained with tears. Lars reached for her and gave her an impulsive hug. "Good work, little sister," he murmured. "Or should I say now, little brother?" His feeble attempt at humor met only a blank stare. Katja was still too raw with grief and fear to respond.

For a few moments, they quietly debated whether they should continue sailing in the sunlight or keep out of sight. After considering the options, Katja said, "Lars, let's continue. It's to our advantage to get as far away from Khartoum as possible, and as long as this breeze continues to blow toward the south, let's use it."

"Very well. Up anchor, and shove off, Katja. Continue sailing we shall." The wind held and the sloop continued its slow journey south on the Blue Nile. Lars and Katja set up a watch program--four hours each at the tiller and four hours to sleep and eat. Occasionally, they spotted Arabs on the west and east banks of the river. They seemed to be farmers tending to their own business and paid little attention to the passing sloop and the escaping pair. Lars and Katja focused their attention on the boat and avoided any eye contact with people on the bank. Katja made a point of keeping her head turned away from those on the shore. She intended that her disguise would protect her from unwanted attention, and she didn't want anyone whose eyes were sharp to look more closely or to challenge them. Most of the time, when she was in her stand-down watch, she tended to miscellaneous chores on deck trying to overcome her chilling fear.

Further up the river, they saw large Nile crocodiles basking in the sun on both sides of the river. Occasionally one of the reptiles swam by the sloop. Sometimes a crocodile nudged the sloop but not with enough force to capsize it. During these occurrences, the two travelers felt a ripple of fear and drew their Webleys to dispatch the reptile if it became too aggressive. In one incident, an extremely large and aggressive crocodile repeatedly shoved the sloop off course and close to the west bank. Katja drew her Webley and was prepared to shoot, but Lars told her to stand down. "Not yet, Katja." Eventually, the beast tired of its game and swam away.

Katja, irritated and fearful, challenged her brother. "Lars, why did you stop me from shooting that reptile? He could have capsized our sloop and that would have been the end of us."

"I was convinced that the croc couldn't do much damage to our large sloop in this calm river. Besides, the sound of a pistol shot would broadcast our position."

Katja, not wholly convinced, began to relax and her fear ebbed. "One of these days, Lars, I'm going to kick your rear end."

"Just wait until we're ashore before you do. I wouldn't care to become lunch for one of these crocs."

Katja gave him a faint smile.

Approaching the first village, they wondered if the Madhi's soldiers would be standing guard and watching river traffic, or whether one of the residents would spot them and sound an alarm. Their fear of discovery and capture welled. In a shaky yet commanding voice, Lars murmured, "Katja, get your rifle and load a round in the chamber. And have your Webley cocked. Be ready to fight. Now, keep down, be quiet, and pull that tarpaulin over you. Probably it's best if you're not seen."

Katja muttered a small pejorative under her breath, then sighed with resignation. With a teasing tone in her voice, she responded, "Aye, aye, sir. As you command, oh mighty Captain Lars Bligh Neufeld."

Lars smiled at her repartee. He realized that Katja's morale was improving, notwithstanding their overarching apprehension of the perils that lay ahead. He chambered a round in his rifle and checked his Webley. As they passed the first village, Lars spotted several Arab boys leading a tribe of goats to the river's bank on the west shore. The boys looked at the passing boat with mild interest then returned to tending their goats. Lars, pretending not to notice them, surreptitiously scanned the village with his binoculars as they sailed past. No one seemed to be about, and he wondered if all the adults were inside their huts or had gone to join the Mahdi.

They passed without incident. About a mile upriver, Lars said with relief in his voice, "Okay, sister. We're safely beyond that village. Come out. All I saw were couple of boys and their goats."

Immediately Katja kicked off the tarpaulin, stood on deck, and holstered her Webley. She was drenched in perspiration and wobbling a little. "Damn, I'm hot and soaking wet, I have a splitting headache, and I'm slightly dizzy." She plopped down on the deck and put her head between her knees.

Lars saw that Katja was perspiring profusely, and the color had drained from her face. He felt her brow: her skin was hot and clammy, and he immediately realized that she was suffering from heat stroke. He rigged the tiller with a rope to hold it steady. "Katja, you're suffering from the heat. Lie down in the sail's shadow. Let me help you get out of those wet clothes."

In a weak and half-joking voice, Katja said, "I need no help. I can remove them by myself, thank you."

Lars gave her a light cotton blanket to cover herself, then went to the food cache and retrieved several items. "Katja, drink this cool water and eat those salt crackers. They'll help rebalance your system." Katja, without looking at Lars, took the victuals and slowly consumed them. Then he opened a can of fruit. Handing her a spoon he commanded, "Eat these peaches and drink all the fluid." She complied weakly. Lars used a packing-box top as a fan to cool her as she lay on the deck.

With maximum effort she looked at Lars, "Thanks, big brother." After a slight pause, "Next time, you get under the tarpaulin and I'll steer."

Katja was manning the tiller. "We'll be passing this next village shortly. Do you recommend that I should hide? Don't even consider the tarpaulin."

"There's no place else to hide. Pull your cap low and stay with the tiller."

They rounded a bend in the river and spotted the village about a mile ahead. Lars scanned the upcoming village with the binoculars. "I don't see any movement. Ease us as far to the east side of the river as possible. Do you have your weapons at the ready?"

Somewhat irritated at the question she thought was patronizing, Katja snapped brusquely, "Of course, big brother. In fact, my Webley is pointed at your rear end."

Chagrinned, Lars responded, "My error." In a second or two, he sprouted a large smile and quipped, "It doesn't matter. You couldn't hit it if you tried."

"Touché."

Lars inwardly breathed a sigh of relief. Katja was recovering her usual good spirits and contributing wholeheartedly to their escape.

The north wind held steady, and the sloop came abreast of the town. Lars scanned it from end to end. He confirmed his initial assessment. "I don't see anyone or any trace of recent activity. The town is probably deserted."

By sunset, the pair had traveled almost one hundred twenty miles. Lars consulted the maps and saw that the Rahad River's confluence with the Blue Nile was about forty-five miles further. "Sister, we're within a day's sailing of the Rahad River. By tomorrow evening, with a fair wind, we should be close to its merger with the Blue Nile. If we're to navigate the confluence at night, we ought to spend tonight near here." He paused to scan the shoreline and spotted a large overhanging tree. "Beach the sloop under that tree, Katja."

"Aye, aye, sir," mocked Katja. Fending away branches, she eased the sloop near the east bank and nosed it into a small cove hidden by the tree. On shore, they faced a shallow, verdant valley surrounded by low-lying brown hills about three hundred yards away. Lars picked up the binoculars, grabbed his rifle, drew his Webley, and jumped ashore. To give covering fire for Lars, Katja slid behind the bow's gunwale and aimed her rifle toward the valley. For the next several minutes, Lars reconnoitered the area. Seeing that there were no humans in the valley, he ran to the hills, dropping to the ground just short of the summit. Using the binoculars, he scanned the vast desert beyond the hills. He did not see anyone or any signs of recent human activity. He waved to Katja. "All clear. Come ashore." Then he hurried back to the riverbank.

Katja tossed the anchor onto the muddy bank and made sure that the flukes was buried. With her rifle slung over her shoulder, she jumped ashore and pulled the sloop's bow up onto the shore. Then, standing with legs apart, she twisted her torso several times to loosen it. She walked several dozen feet toward the hills, cupped her other hand over her eyes, and did a full-circle survey of the area. Convinced that the area was deserted, she grabbed Lars's hand and said, "Walk with me to ease the cramped strain on our bodies."

He raised his left hand in a mock salute. "Very well, Mademoiselle Admiral."

They walked in large circles not far from their sloop. About fifteen minutes in their walk, Katja spoke. "Lars, I've have been wondering. What if one of the Madhi's patrol boats spots us and hails us to heave to?"

Lars stopped, and after a slight pause he responded, "First, I haven't heard that there are such boats on this river. But if one does appear, our sloop can outrun most any boat on this river."

"We can't outrun their bullets!"

"True. If we're challenged, we will not obey. We'll lure them close and then open fire and we'll continue firing until we've killed all on board.

Lars kept his voice calm, but he hadn't forgotten his father's admonition about his duty to Katja in the event of imminent capture. The horror of this possibility made him almost ill. Silently he vowed to double his vigilance. They will not surrender to the Madhi's soldiers.

They spent the rest of the day resting on the bank beside the boat that was tucked under the low-lying branches of a tree. Near sunset, the pair finished their meal. Satiated, Katja said, "I'm so tired I could sleep right here." She stretched out full length, closed her eyes, and sighed deeply.

Lars kicked her shoe lightly. "Not here, sister. Recall Papa's caution about this area. It's too dangerous." He began to pick up the debris they had left from their meal. Katja rose wearily and helped Lars police the area. Satisfied that nothing remained to betray their presence, they returned to the sloop and curled under their blankets. In a few minutes, they were both asleep.

Just as the sun topped the horizon, Lars stirred on his bed of blankets. He started to rise, then halted and without thinking screamed, "Oh, my God!" A deadly mamba was lying next to Katja, absorbing the heat from her body. Its venom is intensely potent and its bite always is fatal.

Katja, aroused by his scream, squirmed in her blanket. The venomous serpent, disturbed by her movement, raised its head and flared its throat, displaying its two fangs and jet-black throat only inches from Katja's neck. It would strike in any second. In his most authoritative voice, Lars commanded softly, "Katja, lie perfectly still. Do not move a muscle."

She mumbled as she propped herself up on one elbow, "What? What are you saying?"

Without responding, Lars grabbed his Webley and with quick and careful aim, he fired. The bullet zipped a few inches from Katja's neck, and the mamba's head flew into the river and its ten-foot headless body collapsed onto Katja.

Katja, now fully awake, in an instant absorbed the scenario. She screamed in horror and collapsed in a dead faint.

Lars's hands shook as he dropped the pistol, grabbed the reptile's body, and tossed it into the river. Then soaking a rag in the water he mopped Katja's brow. He held her and gently rocked her back and forth and whispered words of comfort.

In a minute or so, Katja revived. Understanding that she had been just an instant from a horrible death, she grabbed Lars for support and began to sob. When her sobs quieted, Lars said, "Let's pray that we've overcome the most serious threat facing us." In his heart, however, he knew that more serious perils lie ahead.

After a time, Katja recovered her spirits. "Lars, I'm fine now." She kissed him on the forehead, took his hands in hers, and said with a broad smile, "Thank you, my dear brother, for saving my life." She grabbed him in a bear hug. "I've never been so terrified. That mamba was the devil in disguise after my soul."

Lars smiled and kissed Katja's check.

She returned his smile. As the tension of the moment eased, Katja stood. "We've lingered here far too long. We need to leave. The noise from that shot has broadcast our position. The breeze is brisk, and we need to take advantage of it. I'll rig the sail and man the tiller. You raise the anchor and shove off."

The elevation of the terrain along the river rose slowly, and the scene changed rapidly from desert to savanna to sparsely spaced green meadows spotted with acacia and willow trees. The Blue Nile narrowed slightly, and the river flowed a little faster. Fortunately for the two refugees, the wind remained steady from the north and the sloop progressed at a brisk pace.

Several hours later, Katja spotted an ibex about a hundred yards up the river on its east bank drinking in the Nile. "Lars, loot there! See that ibex at the shore? I see a sumptuous meal waiting for us."

"Yes, I've spotted it." Lars silently retrieved his Martini-Henry rifle, took careful aim, and then he withdrew the rifle from his shooting stance. "Not a practical idea, Katja. I'm going to leave the fellow alone. If I were to fire, we'd give away our position and attract attention."

"Damn, big brother. I was counting on a juicy Ibex steak dinner. But, as usual your judgment is sound." She pauses for a time thinking of the dinner she's missing. "It's hardtack again this evening."

By sundown, they were within a mile of the confluence of the Rahad River and the Blue Nile. With his binoculars, Lars spotted the two towns lying on opposite banks. Studying them carefully, he saw that they appeared to be typical river villages with their residents moving about normally. There was no sign of Muslim soldiers. He tentatively concluded there was nothing to cause alarm. The Nile had narrowed slightly, its banks were higher, and the current was noticeably stronger. The river was muddy and covered with foam as the two rivers mixed. The north wind had increased slightly.

Lars reckoned that with him paddling, they could broach the confluence in about fifteen minutes. He moved the tiller slightly to the right to nudge the sloop into a copse of willows growing along the west bank. "Sister, we'll stay here until sometime after midnight, and then we'll broach the confluence. In the meantime, let's have dinner and sleep."

Much later, low clouds were hiding the crescent of a new moon. Lars wakened his sister and whispered, "Let's move." Katja shook the sleep out of her eyes, took the tiller, and headed the sloop close to the east bank of the Blue Nile to lessen the force of the oncoming Rahad River. With Lars vigorously working a paddle, the sloop made excellent headway. When they hit the confluence, the sloop pitched wildly, and for a moment Katja lost control. The sloop began to swing broadside to the current. The swirling water was much stronger than they had anticipated. Lars paddled with concentrated power to center the boat in the current, and Katja with all her strength swung the tiller opposite the current's push. In a few seconds, they had the sloop pointed upstream again, and it moved forward ever so slowly.

Suddenly the mingling waters calmed and the sloop propelled forward. Soon they were several hundred yards beyond the confluence. Katja pointed the bow toward the east bank to beach the sloop so they could recover their strength. Lars, still panting heavily, commanded, "Sister, keep going. We have to get further upstream. We're too close to those towns." He pushed the paddle deep and steadily into the water. The wind held, and the sloop moved slowly and steadily in the now increasing flow of the Blue Nile as its banks became even narrower and steeper. The low clouds dissipated, and pale moonlight reflected off the swirling river.

Lars drained a canteen, accessed the current, and commented, "Katja, we're too exhausted to continue in this fast-moving river. We should beach the sloop and wait until dawn before we tackle it again. Papa seriously underestimated the dynamics of these two rivers melding."

From her tight face Lars could see that Katja was also feeling the Blue's increasing speed and turbulence. "Agree," she murmured. "This river is getting much harder to navigate. We have to assess our options." Several miles upstream, she beached the sloop in a grove of willow trees. They ate supper, and without a word slipped into their blankets and fell into a weary sleep.

Dawn awakened the pair. The north wind was crisp and still strong. They ate a hurried a repast of canned fruit, cheese, and crackers, and prepared to shove off. Then, glancing at his sister in the fierce light of morning, Lars noticed her pallor.

"Katja, do you have any more of that ink you used on your skin?" Tears, sweat, and cooling splashes of river water had washed away most of her disguise. "You're looking too much like a European."

She reached into one of the duffle bags and pulled out a small bottle of ink and a rag. Lars took them from her and carefully daubed color onto her face and the backs of her hands. It was poor camouflage, but the best they had. It would suffice from a distance, but anyone close to her was certain to notice Katja's delicate features and beardless skin.

The river became swifter and more turbulent as it tumbled down from the highlands. The sloop made tediously slow progress. Lars had been paddling strongly, but it became clear to him that their progress was unsatisfactory. He pulled in his paddle.

"Sister, we're sailing only about three or four miles per hour. I estimate that we've covered no more than ten or eleven miles today. At this rate, it will take us a couple of days to meet the Dinder confluence. I reckon it's about fourteen or fifteen miles upstream."

"And what's your solution, oh mighty admiral?" Katja asked jokingly.

"I'll continue to paddle. You pray and handle the tiller. Keep the sloop close to the east bank where the current is less rapid."

"Aye, aye, admiral." Katja laughed to relieve the tension. She understood that they were fast approaching a critical juncture.

Lars paddled with a constant, forceful rhythm, and the sloop moved slowly and steadily upstream. Soon, he was soaked in perspiration. Katja brought him a canteen of water, and Lars took a long drink. Fortunately, as they progressed upriver the temperature dropped, becoming almost pleasant.

After a couple of hours, Katja realized that Lars needed a break. She beached the boat in a group of low-hanging trees on the east bank. "Thanks, coxswain sister. I need a rest, water, and some of those crackers to replace the salt I've lost." He took his fill and dropped onto a blanket. "Give me a few minutes, and then we'll get underway again."

An hour later Katja awakened Lars with a canteen, a tin of peaches, and a strip of canned beef.

Lars rubbed his eyes and stretched. "I didn't mean to sleep." He accepted Katja's offerings. "Thanks, sister. So far today we've probably covered eight or nine miles." After several moments of reflection, he continued with a touch of frivolity, "Let's keep moving. It's only about sixteen miles to the confluence of the Dinder."

It took a second for Katja to comprehend the irony in his statement. She collapsed in deep laughter. But under the laughter, fear roiled in her soul. Could they complete this dangerous and laborious journey successfully? What would happen if the Madhi's soldiers challenged us? Will I be brave and fight like an angry lioness? What will I do to evade capture? I have heard of the last-bullet option for European women. Do I have the courage for it?" And what of Papa? Is he safe and en route to Bavaria? In an instant, she realized that it was useless to speculate on what her future action might be. Her sterling resolve and keen ingenuity would prevail. Now she had to concentrate on her task of handling the sloop as the river tore at it.

Every mile they sailed up the Blue Nile progress became slower and more difficult. From time to time they passed abandoned and burned-out villages. That morning, an hour or so after they started, they spotted a shepherd with a flock of sheep feeding in the lush grass on the west side of the river, but he gave them no notice. Later, as the sun began to set, the temperature dropped several degrees and low-lying clouds drifted over the river. Lars dropped his paddle in the boat and murmured, "I quit. I'm done. Beach the boat. I can't do any more today."

Katja saw that his face was gaunt with exhaustion. "Lie down." She handed him a canteen, canned fruit, and saltines. Shortly after midnight, the deafening crack of thunder and a lightning strike nearby startled the pair awake. Driving sheets of chilling rain soaked them and the north wind howled. Lars recovered quickly. "Up, Katja! Get up now! We're going to use this driving wind to propel us up this tumultuous river."

Katja moved quickly to the stern, grabbed the tiller, and shouted, "Push off! Rig the mainsail. I have the tiller." The mainsail caught the wind with a loud pop and the sloop catapulted forward. Katja fought to hold the tiller steady. Lars soon joined her and together they managed to bring the sloop under control. The craft rushed through the now foaming river and water washed over its sides.

"Katja, get the bucket and bail. I have the tiller."

Two hours later the storm slackened as it moved southward. The wind slowed and the sloop stalled. It could not overcome the force of the fast moving, slowly rising river. Lars beached the boat, and Katja leaped ashore and pulled the sloop as far up the bank as she could and planted the anchor in the rain-soaked soil.

Lars shouted, "Hang on! I'm coming ashore to help you. We have to get the sloop as far up the bank as we can or else the river will sweep it away."

With the river rising, the bank was now soft mud. With maximum effort the pair pulled the sloop almost completely on shore. Katja planted the anchor's flukes firmly in the rain-soaked ground as far up the bank as the anchor chain would allow.

Soaked, cold, and exhausted, they both fell to the deck. Neither spoke. Lars retrieved the blankets, but they were soaking wet. He shook the water off the tarpaulin and pulled it over them as a cover.

As dawn broke, the sun rose into a bright blue sky laced with high, wispy cirrus clouds. There was a bitter chill in the air. On awaking, Lars emerged from under their tarpaulin shelter and jumped to the ground to check the condition of the sloop. The boat was intact and in no danger of slipping into the river. He and Katja retrieved their abbas from their kit and went to the river's edge. It was roaring past with eddies and swirls, and it was near to overflowing its banks. Tree limbs and miscellaneous jetsam were tumbling swiftly past. Lars studied the river for a short while. "We're not going to sail in that maelstrom," he finally said. "We're stuck here until the river calms."

"Correct as usual, Lars. There's no sense in trying to fight that river. Let's walk around a bit to warm up and to ease the stiffness in our limbs, then I'll set up our camp."

Shortly into their walk Katja blurted, "Lars, we're in a dreadful fix. We can't sail on that turbulent river, and we ought not to stay here. We're perilously vulnerable. If the Madhi's people find us, we'll have no retreat." She walked on for a few seconds, letting her words resonate. "We'll fight. We'll kill as many of those bastards as possible. Those fanatical Muslims will not get me alive." Her chin trembled.

Lars reflected on her words and recalled his father's charge. With dogmatic authority he replied, "You are absolutely correct, Katja." A chill of horror flashed through his body at the prospect of obeying his father's fateful command.

After returning from their walk, Lars studied the maps and checked the surrounding topography. "Sister, we must be close to the confluence with the Dinder River. Can you hear its roar faintly in the distance?"

The pair remained quiet for a few moments. "Perhaps," responded Katja. "The Blue is making so much noise that I can't separate the two sounds. How far away do you think it is?"

"Less than a mile, and more likely much closer. If the view were not blocked by those trees and the undulating terrain, we probably could see it."

Somewhat perplexed, Katja asked, "If the Dinder is so powerful that we can hear it from here, how will we sail across its confluences with the Blue Nile?"

"Excellent question. And my answer is, I have no idea."

Two days later the Nile had subsided appreciably, but the pair concluded that it was still too turbulent to attempt to sail on it. Bored with not much to do, Lars declared, "Sister, I'm going to walk to the Dinder and reconnoiter the confluence, and then move up its north bank to see if there is a portage we can swim across. I'll return about sundown. Meantime, be on guard with your rifle nearby. We have no idea who controls this area."

Uneasy about being left alone in possibly hostile territory but determined to maintain a brave front, Katja replied jocularly in false bravado, "Very well, mighty explorer. I eagerly await your return and report." She rushed to Lars and kissed him on both cheeks. "Please be careful, big brother."

Lars holstered his Webley-455 and snapped a round into his Martini-Henry rifle. As he started, he turned back to Katja. "I'll expect a five-course dinner on my return."

In a few minutes, Lars was at the confluence of the Dinder and Blue Nile rivers. The waters were more turbulent than he had expected. The swift-flowing Dinder rushed helter-skelter into the Blue Nile, producing swirling, debris-choked waters and a deafening roar. A long string of white foam indicated a cataract mid-stream in the Nile. He knew that no matter what, they would have to cross the Dinder in order to remain on the east side of the Blue Nile. With firm resolution, he determined that if he did not find a portage somewhere further up the Dinder, they would have to make their way somehow across the confluence. With a strong wind behind them and his power on the paddle, they just might broach this maelstrom.

Turning away from the confluence, Lars hiked about five miles up the north bank of the Dinder River. The altitude of the terrain was ever increasing, and numerous obstacles slowed his progress—boulders, low hills, and several copses of trees on the steep bank. Looking down on the Dinder, he saw numerous small waterfalls, fast-moving water, and a number of treacherous-looking cataracts. The river roared with a deafening din. So far, there was no passage across it.

Just as Lars was about to return to camp, he tripped on a tree root and slid down a low-lying hill and landed in a large grass-covered meadow. He spotted a hundred-foot waterfall spilling the Dinder into a small lake about one thousand feet long and five hundred feet wide. Perhaps here was a way for Katja and him to swim across this powerful river. He began to walk toward the lake. To his horror, he saw a nest of crocodiles sunning on the near shore. As soon as they saw Lars, they began to stir and several slipped into the lake, daring him to enter.

Dejected that his exploratory hike had not revealed a portage across the Dinder, Lars turned back to camp. He realized that the only way to cross the Dinder was at the confluence. To succeed would take planning, a strong wind, and all the muscle power he had. And a great amount of luck.

Just as Lars came within sight of their camp, the clamor of many hooves alerted him to danger. He spotted a squad of the Madhi's cavalry bearing down on him. He began to run as fast as he could and reached the camp about the same time as the cavalry. He did not see Katja. *Where is she?* he wondered in panic. Had the Arabs already captured her?

"Halt!" shouted the squad leader. "Drop that Englishman's rifle." All four members of the troop had their weapons trained on him.

Lars turned to face them, placed his rifle on the ground, and raised his hands in surrender.

The squad leader ordered his troop of three soldiers to dismount and take their captive under control. Mounted on his Arabian steed, he confronted Lars. "Who are you?" he demanded. "What are you doing in this remote location? Why do you run from us? Answer me now."

Lars realized that he had no choice but to respond. He thought that perhaps he could mislead them with his language skills and Arab garb. He looked at the leader. "Al-salaam aleikum." He bowed and touched his heart and forehead in the traditional greeting. "I am Mohammed Abdul-Hafeez of Sennar, scouting for a company of dervishes to cross this devil of a river. So far, I've had no success. Are you familiar with this area? Do you know of any place where those soldiers can cross?" Lars's heart was pounding, but he decided that his best hope lay in controlling the direction of the encounter. Cautiously he scanned the camp for a sign of Katja.

The squad leader studied him carefully. "So, you are a soldier of the Mahdi? To which emir's flag are you pledged? And tell me why that large boat is docked near your camp. It is a European boat, is it not?"

Caught by the unexpected questions, Lars stood silently and could not respond promptly with coherent answers.

The squad leader dismounted and drew his scimitar. Standing only a foot or so in front of Lars, he pointed the scimitar at his captive's midsection and growled, "You are a fake. Your countenance and dress pretend to tell me that you are one of my comrades in the Madhi's holy struggle. But you are not my comrade." He moved his scimitar threateningly as if to slash Lars. "Your accent, manner, and lies betray you. You are European, even though you look and dress as an Arab. Only high-ranking officers are allowed to have English rifles. And certainly you are not a Muslim. Put your hands behind your back so I can tie them. I am taking you to our camp for a comprehensive interrogation."

The sharp crack of rifle fire disrupted the scene. One of the scouts dropped dead with a hole leaking blood in his forehead. In quick succession, two more shots dropped the remaining Mahdi soldiers.

Distracted by the firing, the squad leader turned to see where the sniper was hiding. Lars, seizing the opportunity, drew his Webley and put a round in the back of the leader's head.

From the riverbank came a shaky female voice. "Are they dead? All of them?" Katya emerged over the bank, the Martini-Henry rifle in her hand. With a deep sigh of relief, Lars realized that Katja was safe and had just rescued him. He checked the bodies. "These martyrs are in their heaven enjoying the celestial virgins." To relieve the tension he mocked, "I don't know how. Their bodies lie here."

Katja rushed to Lars. From lying on the river's edge, her clothes were muddy and soaking wet. He grabbed her in a big hug and kissed her on both cheeks. Tears formed in his eyes. "My dear, loving sister, thank you for saving my life. When I entered our camp and saw that you weren't here, I was alarmed that those soldiers had captured you."

"Not hardly, big brother. When I heard them coming, I grabbed my rifle and hid in the river behind our sloop's stern. I saw you running and vowed that those Mahdi soldiers would not capture you or me. I was prepared to fight to the end." She took several deep breaths to relieve her tension. "Now, let's get to work and dump these bodies into the river."

After their gruesome task was completed, Katja wiped her hands on her thobe several times as if to erase her sacrilegious deed. To ease her disquiet she flippantly said, "The crocodiles downriver will have an excellent dinner this evening."

As the pair walked back to their camp, Katja remarked thoughtfully, "I've never even shot at a living creature, much less tried to kill another person. I should be shaking, guilt-ridden, and remorseful. But I feel exhilarated and proud that I have removed three of those bastards from this planet." She walked about a bit. "Where is my guilt for taking three of God's children?" she asked. "Can God forgive me?"

Lars watched his sister in wonder. He saw an unfamiliar strength in her movements and heard a new fierceness in her voice. His genteel, convent-educated sister was gone. A heroic woman was emerging from the crucible of their ordeal.

Returning to the tasks at hand, Katja said, "Let's spook the horses to run away."

"No, Katja. Keep the horses here."

Katja looked at Lars with questioning eyes.

"If we send these horses away, they'll return to their camp with empty saddles. The senior officer will wonder what happened to his scouts and will send patrols to find them. And they'll probably find us as we wait for the river to subside."

Katja, with a quick facetious retort, "As usual, big brother, you're right. I'll get the horses and tie them off to the sloop."

After few minutes Katja commanded, "Turn around. I'm getting out of these wet clothes and wrapping myself in a blanket."

Lars cocked his head questioningly.

"Don't look at me that way. I have to wash the mud off this thobe. Even if it's dirty afterward, it won't be worse than what most of the peasants wear. Remember, we have to look like we belong here. So far it has concealed my fore and aft curves admirably." She began to pull off the thobe. "While I'm busy with the laundry, lay out the food for our dinner."

That evening there was a beautiful sunset. The wind was calm, and the chill intensified. The pair, snug in their abbas, sat by the dying campfire. Katja was in deep thought as she stared at the velvety red sky. Finally, as the sun slipped below the horizon, she dolefully commented, "Our troubles keep compounding. Every step we take is fraught with increasing danger. We're on a fool's journey, and my fear nearly overwhelms me. How much longer can I keep up this bravado?" She dropped her head to her knees and tears slid down her cheeks. In a few seconds, she recovered and said, "Excuse me, big brother. I know absolutely that we had to escape Khartoum. There was no other choice." She dabbed at her tears and was silent for a few moments.

Lars took Katja in his arms and rocked her gently back and forth. "I'm here with you, dear sister. I'll protect you with all my strength and will. And you will support me with your dauntless courage, hard work, and good cheer. Working together, we'll complete this journey." He forced himself to sound confident, but in his heart, he shared Katja's fears.

"Lars, yes, we'll do this together." She wiped her last tears away, stood, and walked a few feet. "Lars, you and I will succeed. But I'm so worried about Papa. "Did he escape? Have the Muslims captured him? Is he alive? Will we ever be united again as a family?

"Katja, we cannot know Papa's fate. To focus on it distracts us from our primary goal. In a few minutes, Katja murmured, "My speculation about Papa's fate burns my soul but I realize that it is counterproductive. There's nothing we can do to help him. He believed in our strength and determination. We have to go on and live up to his faith in us." She took a deep breath. "We will prevail and Papa will be proud of us."

"You're doing just that, Katja. Papa would be so impressed by your courage and strength."

She stared at the ashes of the dead campfire and walked about to recover her composure. Turning back to Lars, she spoke with a steady voice. "Tell me about your reconnaissance trip up the Dinder."

"I hiked about five miles along the river and saw no way for us to cross it. I did find a small lake at the base of a towering waterfall. We might have been able to swim across it, but that's not practical. It's infested with crocodiles."

Katja sat and tucked her arms under her knees. "What now, brother? How do we get to the other side of the Dinder and stay on the east side of the Blue Nile?"

"We have two options. We have to try to broach the confluence. And if we can't do that, we beach our sloop on the west side of the Blue, salvage what stores we can carry, cut our boat loose and let the river destroy it, and we proceed on foot."

Katja lets the concept of traveling on the west side turn over in her mind. "Walking on the west side at this point courts serious danger. The holy city of Sennar is only about twenty miles from here. The entire west side is probably infested with devout Muslims eager to enslave or murder all the Westerners in the Sudan."

"Correct." Lars carefully formed his next comment. "We don't know if the Nile is navigable beyond the confluence. Also, we have to consider that if we do broach the confluence, we'll be cornered between the Blue Nile and the Dinder. Without any information about the geography of the terrain up ahead, it's possible that we could be trapped by an impassable barrier, either by a land form or more raging waters."

Katja stood and walked about evaluating Lars's options. "The alternatives you outline are fraught with manifold perils, but I can't think of any action less dangerous." She sat directly in front of Lars and looked him straight in his eyes. "What is your recommendation?"

With reservation Lars answered, "We try to broach the confluence. It won't be easy, but it's the only option we have for the best long-term outcome. The immediate peril is that if the river turns our sloop broadside to the current we'll be swamped. We'll be swept downstream by the swirling water, our supplies will be lost, and the sloop will be wrecked. And we'll probably drown and become dinner for those crocodiles downstream."

With mocking scorn, Katja raised her voice. "Damn, big brother, you're a perfect fountain of tragic doom. What demons have possessed you? None of those options is attractive." She cracked a broad smile. "Nonetheless, I understand, and I favor broaching the confluence."

After a slight pause, she grabbed Lars's arm. "Brother, be my strength to overcome my fears."

Lars sat silently for a long moment. He had been wrestling with his own fears, and he shared Katja's concerns for their future. At moments—when his shoulders screamed with pain from working the boat's paddle, when he was trying to decipher the maps and plot out their course, when he awoke in the night damp with the cold perspiration of fear—he cursed the fate that had exiled him from his comfortable home and beloved father. He didn't want the burden of leading this terrifying expedition of escape, and he didn't want to face the all-too-likely consequences of capture. At times he wanted to scream with frustration and rage at their situation. But he knew that his father's charge to them was the best possibility they had of survival in a world gone mad, that he had no choice but to continue onward as best he could.

He took a deep breath to calm himself. Then, in the steadiest voice he could manage, he replied firmly, "Then it's settled. Tomorrow afternoon when the wind is strongest, we'll try. In the morning, we'll rig a light blanket as a bowsprit. We're going to need all the force we can muster."

Late the following afternoon, Katja, with difficultly in the fast-moving river, beached the sloop a short distance south of the Dinder's confluence on the east side of the Blue Nile. Lars stowed the paddle. He was soaked in sweat, breathing hard, and totally exhausted. The muscles in his arms screamed with pain, and he collapsed into the bottom of the sloop. Soaking a towel in the cool river water, Katja mopped Lars's face and kissed his cheek. "God love you, my dear brother. You did it! With God-inspired resolve and your heroic power, we're on the south side of the confluence."

Lars was too fatigued to respond coherently and grunted an acknowledgement. Images of his arduous fight with the Blue Nile flashed through his mind. Several minutes later, his strength and resolve began to return. He sat up and greedily gulped water from a canteen, drinking his fill. Then he slumped back down in the sloop.

Katja knew that they must continue to move southward to get away from the dangerous mixing of the two rivers that they had just successfully broached. She rigged the sails, pulled in the anchor, and pointed the bow upstream. The wind had eased and the Blue Nile flowed fast and turbulent in its narrow channel. Once in the stream, Katja could not make headway. In fact, she found it difficult even to hold her position. She quickly beached the boat again and tossed the anchor onto the east bank. "Lars, we're stuck! The wind has failed us. The current is too swift. If we attempt to sail up this river, it will push us back downstream into the cauldron of that confluence. We don't have enough power to overcome the river's brute force." With increasing anxiety she cried, "We can't go forward, and we can't remain here." She began to shiver in disquiet as she realized their peril and that Lars's extraordinary effort was for naught. Already the power of the river was tearing hard at their sloop to propel it backward into the maelstrom.

Lars rallied what strength and resolve he had left. "Katja, we have to get to the west bank." He saw that the Nile here was only about twenty-five feet wide. As he crawled to the bow, he told Katja, "Put the tiller slightly to the right to point the bow to the west bank and hold it with all your might. We dare not get broadsided."

"Very well."

Lars hauled in the anchor and immediately the river pushed the sloop backward. Mustering all his power, he hurled the anchor high in the air, and it sailed over the west bank. It landed and the flukes took a firm purchase in the soft mud. He circled the chain around the mast for a more powerful pulling position and overhanded the chain slowly pulling the sloop to the bank.

"Get out, Katja! Grab your kit, weapons, and all the supplies you can. I can't hold this position for long—a minute or two at best. This current is damnable."

With her arms full, Katja jumped into the bank and scrambled to safety on the shore above. Grabbing the anchor chain, she dug her heels into the mud and held it with all her strength.

With the river tearing at the sloop, Lars grabbed his kit, weapons, some supplies, and leaped onto the steep bank. Katja extended her hand, helping him climb to safety. Once Lars was on the shore behind the bank, she hurled the anchor into the sloop. Immediately the raucous river propelled the boat into the confluence. It smashed into the rocks in the cataract, broke into splinters, and disappeared as just so much jetsam.

Soaked with Nile water, the dejected pair sat in silence. The late afternoon winds were growing stronger, and they shivered in the cool air. They were on the west side of the Blue Nile, where they ought not to be. Their sloop was wrecked, and most of their supplies were in the river. After some time, Katja broke the silence. "What now, big brother? Do we sit here out in the open all night or do we get moving?"

Lars rose, picked up his kitbag, and hitched it onto his back. "Up, little sister. You're right. We can't remain here. That copse of trees atop that low hill will give us some shelter and cover, and we'll make a camp there."

For the next two days, the pair traveled quietly and shadow-like in the thick forest. They circled several miles west of Sennar, and gave wide margins around the Madhi's warriors standing guard at crossroads. From, time-to-time they spotted Arabs and Nubians who were either tending flocks or walking to or from Sennar. These Africans seemed not to have seen the pair. Lars commented, "So far, little sister, our luck holds."

Katja responded, "Perhaps you're correct. But Abyssinia is a long walk from here, and this forest cover won't last forever. Sooner or later we'll be traveling in the open.

"We'll adapt when we get there. So far, we've probably walked twenty miles, maybe twenty-five, perhaps more."

Katja made a quick calculation and quipped in a mocking voice, "Indeed, Lars, we have only a hundred more miles or so to reach Abyssinia." Then in a more serious tone, "And even then we won't be entirely safe. The slave trade is flourishing again, and the slavers' source of supply is the black tribes close to the border."

Lars continued to lead their pace, "Yes, Katja."

Four days later the pair spent the night at the edge of the forest. Ahead lay a vast savanna dotted with a few straggly thorn trees. On their left, the Blue Nile was fast moving and roaring as it plunged down from the Abyssinian highlands. With no other choice, the pair continued their hike, carefully avoiding a caravan track not far from the river.

The next morning, a sharp sting on Lars's chest awakened him. He bolted upright and saw an Arab with his scimitar pointed at his heart. Ten other Arabs, with their rifles drawn, surrounded the pair.

"Get up!" shouted the Arab. "What are you doing here? Tell me who you are."

Lars stood up proudly and answered in his most confident and authoritative voice, "I am Mohammed Abdul-Hafeez, and my brother and I are returning to our village in the hills after we've sold our goats in Sennar."

The hubbub awakened Katja. She saw what was happening and reached for her pistol tucked under her blanket. A scimitar slashed down a few inches from her hand. She quickly pulled her hand away and realized with incredulous horror that the Arabs had captured them. She was helpless with no way to fight. Her expression was taut and drained. She quickly recovered her resolve and stared at her adversary with unbridled hatred.

Lars pretended not to notice Katja and continued his dissembling. "We are shepherds and bother no one."

The leader gazed at Lars coldly, "Before you continue, I should introduce myself." He placed his hands on his hips and with a swagger announced, "I am Pasha Zobeir Rahamma. I am a slaver of great reputation. General Gordon called me 'notorious.' Perhaps you have heard of me?"

Stunned at being confronted by the most infamous of all the slavers, Lars nodded and in a soft voice replied, "Yes, I know who you are."

"Very well." Zobeir walked around Lars, taking his mettle. "Abdul-Hafeez, you are a liar. Your story is false. My people control this area, and they spotted you and this boy several days ago. You did not come from Sennar. You came from somewhere north of this city. And I find it most curious that you avoided entering this holy city. In fact, my men tell me that you were careful to avoid it by walking several miles west of it. They have waited to seize you until I returned from Abyssinia with my captives. See those blacks in choke chains--almost one hundred of them from the Shifa tribe. I am taking them to the slave market in Omdurman. You and your brother will join them."

Guards grabbed Lars and snapped a choke chain around his neck, then pushed him to the ground. Helpless and confounded, he was realizing his worst fear—he could do nothing to save Katja.

Almost on cue, one of Zobeir's guards grabbed Katja's shoulders and jerked her up to a standing position. He bound her hands behind her back with a wire rope. She turned and with all her strength, she kicked him in the groin. He crumbled to the ground moaning in acute pain.

Zobeir slapped Katja with all his might and she staggered backward and fell to the ground. Her left cheek turned blood red and a large, ugly welt rose across it. "Boy, you need to understand that I do not tolerate insubordination. You are my prisoner." He grabbed and pulled her upright, then struck her across her back with his whip. Katja cried in pain and stumbled to the ground. Zobeir flailed her again and again. She curled up in the fetal position for protection from the whip and tried not to give Zobeir satisfaction by crying out. But the pain was too intense and relentless, and she screamed and screamed. Flooded with pain, she vaguely knew that her worst fear was upon her.

Lars shouted, "Stop! Stop! Take your anger out on me, not my brother." "Stand up, boy," demanded Zobeir. "I might give you to the guard you assaulted. That is, if he is able." He roared with laughter at his obscene joke.

Trying to obey, Katja attempted to rise but could not. With her hands tied behind her back, she could not find support, and her beaten body would not cooperate. She almost got up on one knee but without leverage, she stumbled to the ground. Immediately one of the guards seized her, threw her upright, and said, "There is more of that whip to come if you do not behave." The lingering pain was so severe, and her mind so cloudy, that she could not reply coherently. She nodded her head affirmatively.

Zobeir looked carefully at Katja. "How old are you, boy?"

"Eighteen," Katja whispered through her pain.

"Hmmm." Zobeir walked around her. "Under all that dirt, you're a pretty little fellow, aren't you?" He smiled and turned away. "I suspect you'll fetch a nice price at the slave market. I have some clients with rather...specialized tastes." He smiled more broadly. "Yes, a nice price indeed."

Zobeir went to Lars. "You, get up off the ground." He circled Lars, all the while staring at him with his steely black eyes. With his head cocked questioningly, he asked Lars, "Who are you? Tell me the truth, or I shall flay your brother alive." He continued circling Lars.

Lars, totally defeated, said, "I am Lars Neufeld from Khartoum, and this is my brother." Making a desperate attempt to maintain their charade, he said, "His name is Karl." He told Zobeir about their escape from Khartoum and adventures up the Blue Nile.

Zobeir listened patiently then smiled broadly. "So, young Neufeld, after all your efforts to escape the Mahdi's forces, you have fallen into my hands. You should consider yourself fortunate. Unlike some of my compatriots, I see much more value in your living bodies than in the destruction of your immortal souls." He snorted cynically. "You're too dark and rough-looking to be sold for much more than heavy labor, but your brother here—well, I know of several very wealthy customers with a taste for pretty boys."

Zobeir nodded to the guard Katja had assaulted, now somewhat recovered. "Strip this lad and let us see what prize we have."

The guard used his scimitar to cut away what remained of Katja's whip-slashed clothes.

When Zobeir saw Katja's feminine body he burst into loud laughter. "Blessed be Allah!" he gasped through his guffaws. "This is an even greater prize." Then he realized that Katja's deep tan covered only her face and hands. "A European lady! Oh, Allah has truly blessed me today."

Then Zobeir spotted the jewelry and gold coins taped to her body. "And the blessings just keep on coming! We indeed have a rare prize here. Free her hands, and strip those trinkets from her and bring them to me."

Katja had turned her face away from her captor and tried to cover herself with her arms and hands. Realizing this was impossible, she summoned all the courage and physical stamina she had and stood defiantly naked in front of her captors with her body proudly erect. Large, crisscrossed red whip welts covered her torso, arms, hands, and legs. Her feet were slightly apart, her arms akimbo, fists clenched, shoulders square, head high, and chin thrust forward, and her eyes shot fiery venom at Zobeir.

Lars cringed away from the sight of his sister's shame. He turned his head and closed his eyes. It was too late, he knew, to fulfill his father's final charge and save his sister's honor from the ignominy and horror that lay ahead for her. He felt nauseous with shame and fear.

Zobeir's eyes enlarged as he lustily perused every part of Katja's near-perfect body. "Are you married?"

Katja, her heart racing and trembling inside, refused to answer. Zobeir flexed his whip with a loud crack just in front of her. "Are you married, white woman?"

Katja stood perfectly still and continued her stare of unbridled hatred. "So you want to feel my whip again." He raised his whip to strike Katja. Lars shouted, "No, she's not married."

Zobeir turned to Lars. "How did you come to have this woman with you? Is she your captive, or are you hers? Be truthful, or I'll flog both of you."

"She's my sister."

"Sister? But you're an Arab. How do you come to have a European sister?"

Lars explained their background and his role as adopted son.

With exuberance in his voice, Zobeir declared, "So, we have captured a beautiful young European virgin! Today Allah blesses me with extra good fortune. Once I get her cleaned up, she will fetch an enormous price at the slave market for this rare opportunity." He smiled broadly and rubbed his hands together with glee. "In frenzied bidding, emirs, pashas, viziers, and sheiks will empty their gold purses to possess her." He roared with pleasure. "Indeed! She will be the coveted prize in any harem." After a few minutes, he ordered a guard to give Katja a caftan.

Without acknowledgement, she slipped on the foul-smelling, louse-infested garment. The raw wool rubbing across her whip welts only increased her pain and distress.

Zobeir addressed Lars. "You also have treasures taped to your body? Take off your clothes." Lars complied, and the slaver stripped the jewels and gold from his body. "My good fortune increases many-fold. Indeed, this has been a most fortuitous day." He ordered one of his men to put a choke collar on the woman and chain the two new prisoners together. "I personally will lead these Westerners to Omdurman." He ordered his troop to move out, and they headed north toward Sennar.

Zobeir and several of his men rode on camels; the others patrolled the long line of slaves. Their progress was slow because the blacks, in their heavy chains, could not move quickly. Even the crack of the Arabs' whips was powerless to increase the pace of the caravan. Lars and Katja were tied by a ten-foot rope to Zobeir's camel, and they struggled to keep pace. Several times Katja fell and was dragged several feet before Zobeir stopped. "Keep up, woman." He used his whip again. Katja, with all the resolve she could muster, refused to acknowledge her pain. She was determined not to give her captor the satisfaction of acknowledging his power over her.

"You have spirit, white woman. Good. Such bravery will bring even a better price for you. My buyers revel in breaking the spirit of their slaves--especially the females."

Lars tried to interfere, but a guard knocked him to the ground. Zobeir stood over him. "If you try that again, I will flog you until your sister begs me to take her. Are we clear?"

That evening the Arabs made camp on a slight rise in the plain. The guards handed out a gruel of some sort and a container of foul water to the prisoners. Lars and Katja, resigned to their fate, huddled together in the chill night air. The iron collars had chafed their necks raw. They did not speak, and sleep came as a relief from their tortuous day.

Later in the night when the moon was full, Lars and Katja were awakened by a terrifying ruckus: gunfire, screams, shouts, the whinnies of terrified horses. Almost as quickly as it began, there was quiet. Lars and Katja sat up to see what was happening. Katja emitted a sharp cry when she saw a huge black man standing over them with his bloody sword ready to strike.

Lars cried, "We're prisoners! Prisoners just like the Nubians."

The fellow stooped and fingered their choke collars. "So I see. Get up." Lars and Katja complied with his command. Still wondering what had happened, Lars asked, "Who are you?" Looking at the chaotic scene, he continued, "What happened? Where are the Arab guards and Zobeir?"

"So many questions from slaves in chains." The fellow carefully inspected the pair--an Arab and a white woman. "I am curious to know your story. Tell me later perhaps." He stared at the pair with deeply-questioning eyes. With a grunt of satisfaction, he answered, "First, I am Shaiqiya, guardian of the Shifa tribe. I and my friends have rescued my people from these slavers."

Lars saw that their rescuer was husky and much taller than the Arabs. He had a ready smile enhanced by almond-shaped, jet-black eyes.

Shaiqiya continued, "The guards now are martyrs and are in their heaven. Zobeir, the coward, scurried away on his camel at the first shot. In his tent was this cache of gold coins and rare jewels. They are yours, I presume?"

"Yes, that is correct. Zobeir took them from us yesterday when he captured us."

"Then I am pleased to return them to their rightful owners."

Shaiqiya stared at Katja. "And who is this white woman? Your slave?"

Katja, replied in the firmest voice she could muster, "I am not a slave. At least not now that you have rescued us." On reflection, she asked with a worried brow, "Are you going to make us your slaves?"

Shaiqiya began to laugh. "Not hardly, young lady. I am a Christian from our ancient city of Ankobar, and I have pledged virtue to God through our Orthodox Bishop of Addis Ababa. As you see, I have saved my people and you from that horrible institution with which the Muslims have plagued my people for years. Now we fight back."

In the interim, Shaiqiya's soldiers had freed their brothers, gathered the Arab spoils, and were ready to move.

Some weeks later, Lars and Katja had concluded their audience with the King of Abyssinia, Ras Gugsa Yejice, in Addis Ababa. He guaranteed them safe passage to the border with British East Africa. At the border, a colonial administrator escorted them to Nairobi, where the British colonial governor-general, Sir William Mackinon, OBE, greeted them as honored guests. He arranged an escort for them to the German protectorate Equatoria in East Africa. The German *chargé d'affaires* in Nairobi sent a telegram to the governor of Equatoria, Pasha Eduard Schnitzer, advising him of Lars's and Katja's impending arrival in Dar-es-Salaam.

It was now September 1886, a year and a half since Lars and Katja fled Khartoum. Fully recovered from their ordeal, they were comfortably ensconced in a hotel in Dar-es-Salaam. One afternoon in their hotel's bar they sipped German lager in large tankards and made plans for their future.

With a sigh, Katja placed her tankard on the table. "Lars, we've lingered here far too long. We need to leave and get to Bavaria, try to find Papa, and meet our relatives. I've checked with the Hamburg-Bremen Afrika Line's shipping office, and they have a tramp steamer with space for four passengers bound for Bremerhaven leaving in seven days. I'll purchase our tickets." With a big smile of anticipation, she took a long swallow of her beer.

Lars looked down at the table in front of him. With a struggle in his voice he raised his eyes to meet Katja's. "My dear loving sister, I've decided to remain here in Equatoria. I have an offer from the governor to help form a bureau to coordinate and help the many refugees in this country. I'm an African and an Arab; my future is in Africa. I would not assimilate in a white European country. Here, I can do more to help Africans." He dropped his eyes in shame for deceiving his sister.

Shocked and unbelieving, Katja stared at Lars. "You're not serious? Not after all we've been through in our escape, all our love growing up together, and our father's charge to immigrate to Germany!" But in her wounded heart, she knew that Lars was serious. Tears fell on her cheeks.

"Katja, I've known of my decision for several days but had not the opportunity or courage to tell you. My love for you is unbounded, and I shall miss you terribly. We bonded as no other brother and sister ever have. We'll always have our love, and the experiences of our escape are imprinted on our souls. But I must start my new life here."

Through her sobs Katja whispered, "Very well, Lars. I understand and accept your decision, but I'm painfully hurt and I shall miss your love, and your shield."

Fifteen years later, Katja was married, had three strong, growing sons, and lived in Augsburg, Bavaria. Her husband was a major in the Kaiser's First Royal Bavarian Heavy Cavalry. Over the years, she and Lars exchanged frequent newsy letters. Notwithstanding their many letters to various governments in Africa, neither had any information about their father. His fate was unknown. This year Katja decided to write a story about their escape from the Madhi's terror in the Sudan. For a resolution of their journey to freedom, she needed to know what happened to her father. As a last resort, she wrote a letter to the German ambassador in Cairo and implored him to make a concerted effort to solve this riddle.

A couple of months later, Katja received a cablegram from the German chargé d'affaires in Khartoum. "I have researched all possible resources to find any trace of your father, the jeweler Dieter Neufeld. I am sorry to report that there is no record of him after 1885. Nothing remains of his shop at the address you have provided. Nowadays, that site is a haberdashery run by an English tailor. Accordingly, I must assume that your father perished in the chaos of the Madhi's rape of Khartoum. I am saddened to bring such bad news. My duty requires that I declare the German citizen Dieter Neufeld deceased. I am sending you his death certificate by separate post."

Katja folded the letter carefully and put it in the letter drawer in her desk. After so many years, she had almost expected this response. She drafted a letter to send this news to Lars.

Two months later, she received Lars's response. He was not surprised at the diplomat's conclusion. It was as he had assumed. He closed his long letter with the news that he has joined the Territorial Reserve Army and had the rank of Sergeant First Class. He concluded, "With the deterioration of diplomatic negotiations between the major powers in Europe and the threat of war looming large, I must do my duty as a loyal German to defend our fatherland. Long live Kaiser Wilhelm."

FIN

About S. Martin Shelton

Captain Shelton retired from active and reserve naval service several years ago. He was a photojournalist skilled in several facets of his profession and has an extensive background in Soviet and Chinese studies. He served in the Korean and Vietnam wars. His duties required that he travel throughout the world and with particular emphasis on the Far East.

Shelton earned his Bachelor of Science degree (Physics) from St. Mary's University, San Antonio, and his Master of Arts in Cinema from the University of Southern California. For several years, he produced a host of information motion-media shows, winning over forty awards in national and international film competitions and festivals. He was elected a fellow of the Society for Technical Communication and the Information Film Producers of America.

Shelton has published extensively in trade magazines, peer-reviewed journals, and commercial publications. After retirement from the Naval Reserve, he completed his book *Communicating Ideas with Film, Video, and Multimedia,* which earned the Best of Show award in a major publication competition. He continued his writing by publishing his first novel *St. Catherine's Crown.* In addition to the published books noted in this blog, he continues to write on his favorite subjects: historical fiction of the near past, monographs on documentary film/video production, photography, and ghost-towns of the west.

Please flip book to enjoy a second story.

The Pope IN ROME RANSOMS A CHRISTIAN KNIGHT from a gruesome Muslim prison. By a Holy Writ, the Pope charges him to search Asia to find the chimerical Prester John and bring him to Rome to pay tribute from his fabulously wealthy kingdom. This narrative recounts the knight's decades-long hazardous adventures in search for this mythical prince.

Prester John

Inquiries should be addressed to the Publisher
Lamplight Press
PO Box 82516,
Austin, Texas 78708

ISBN: 978-0-9892861-8-3

Printed in the United States of America

One

I am Giovanni Benito Cosimo, a knight of the Sovereign Military Hospitaller Order of Saint John of Jerusalem of Rhodes and of Malta. My chronicle begins in early 1187 when I answered Pope Clement III's command for the Christian kings of Europe to form the Third Crusade. The Pope's charge was to recapture the Holy Land from the Muslim Saladin and his Saracens, rescue the Holy Sepulcher, and restore Jerusalem as the holy site of Christendom. I sailed from Naples bound for Malta to meet with other Knights of Saint John.

Before we proceed, perhaps I ought to discuss my background. The nuns at the orphanage told me I was born in May 1169 in the small town of Padova—a few miles west of Venice. My unwed mother abandoned me in a pew in the Cathedral of the Assumption of the Blessed Virgin Mary. The kind nuns of The Order of Saint Francis took me to their orphanage. They raised and educated me to become a physician. At seventeen, however, I left the orphanage to answer the Doge of Venice's, Orio Mastropiero, call for soldiers to fight the Croatian pirates who had been raiding the Venetian cities throughout the Adriatic Sea. For reasons I do not understand, I had a natural affinity for fighting. In several battles, I distinguished myself with heroic actions. After our victory, the Doge, a viceroy in the Sovereign Military Hospitaller Order of Saint John of Jerusalem of Rhodes and of Malta, knighted me in St. Mark's Cathedral. Since then, I have been searching for commissions to earn my living in the name of our Christian God.

In our small fleet bound for Malta were twenty other knights, their squires, bowmen, pikemen, horses, and the paraphernalia needed for war. A few days after departing Malta, we arrived in Rhodes where we joined compliant kings and thousands of knights from the Christian kingdoms.

Under the command of Richard I, whom we called Coeur de Lion because of his distinguished valor, I fought in successful battles in Palestine where we captured the coastal cities of Acre, Arsuf, and Jaffa. In 1190, I was posted to the besieged city of Tyre in Syria. Conrad of Montferrat was in command of the Christian forces defending the city. Several thousand skilled Saracen warriors surrounded us. Their siege weapons hurled solid projectiles that pounded the walls and flaming projectiles that started conflagrations within the city. Their bombardment was without respite.

Realizing that without relief, we could not endure indefinitely, Conrad ordered me to lead a large force to counterattack. Our goal was to break through the Saracens' lines to capture an oasis about three miles to the south. From this oasis, we were to sortie and harass the Saracens from their rear thus easing pressure on the city. In just a matter of minutes after leaving the South Gate, I realized that we were doomed. My troop fell in droves to a fusillade of arrows, and from projectiles launched from the Saracens' mangonels. Discipline disintegrated, and in a chaotic frenzy, my men broke in disorder. To the man, the Saracens cut them down.

A projectile pummeled me on the head. From the gaping wound, blood flooded my eyes, nose, mouth, and down my neck onto my chest. As the world became blacker and blacker, I staggered to the ground unconscious. I lay comatose all day among the dead, dying, and moaning wounded.

Shortly after sunrise, squads of victorious Muslim soldiers scoured the battlefield to recover their dead for prompt burial and to collect Christian spoils: weapons, armor, trophies, and prisoners. I lay semiconscious and barely aware of my wound or my surroundings. My only sensation was the pounding pain in my head. The blazing sun and a sharp pain in my neck stimulated my awareness. A Saracen had a scimitar at my throat and was demanding that I renounce Christianity and embrace Mohammedanism, which he insisted was the only true religion. I had no voice to respond with my resounding rejection. Such silence probably saved my life. His cohorts ripped the large silk red cross off my white outer garment and ground it into the sand. I relapsed into unconsciousness and have no recall of the next events.

Sometime later, I do not know how many days had passed, I regained my full senses. My first sensation was to realize that there was no pain in my head. I discovered that I was lying on a stone floor in a dark place. Someone had washed the blood from my body and bandaged my wound. Slowly, I realized I was in a Saracen prison. My worst fear overwhelmed me.

I was in solitary confinement in a cell with no windows. The only light came through a small window with iron bars in the heavy door. I had no way to distinguish between night and day or to keep track of the passing days. The Saracen guards were my only human contact. Soon, boredom tore at my soul. I do not know how long I was so confined. Prayer was my only solace.

After a time, the warden came to my cell. I rose from the straw scattered on the floor to face him as his rules demanded. "Christian knight," he said, "You have caused me no trouble. If you agree to obey scrupulously all my rules, I will grant you parole. You may mingle with my other prisoners and have access to the few books we have. Understand, any violation of my rules brings severe punishment. Do you accept?"

Stunned at this generous offer, I stumbled, "Yes warden, I accept." I paused for a few seconds as I explored the possibilities in his offer, "In Venice I was a medical student. Perhaps I could be of assistance to the other prisoners and even to your guards."

He raised his right eyebrow and advanced toward me. "Christian knight if this is a ploy you will not live to see it through. If you are sincere, do what you can."

I was helpless. There were no medicines, instruments, or bandages to alleviate the pain and disease of my fellow prisoners. At best, I could only give consolation and empathy. To challenge my mind, I began to learn Arabic. In a few months, I was fluent. I could read, write, speak, and understand this Oriental language. I was surprised that I learned my guards' language so quickly. I had no idea that I had an affinity for languages. I began to study the different dialects of our jailers who came from many sections of the vast Muslim empire. I even mastered Farsi, the language of Persia. My fellow prisoners tasked me to be their interpreter and spokesman.

Be not deceived. There was no hope. The prison warden ruled by the whip. Any violation of his absurd and inflexible rules incurred a flogging. The screams of knights as the lash ripped into their backs permeated our cells and assaulted our ears. On three occasions, I myself felt the lash for minor infractions—to this day the scars remain. Branding and amputations were the punishments for serious violations. Rations were short—the food was putrid and frequently maggot-infested, and the water was stale and malodorous. We were dying slowly of torture, prison rot, malnutrition, disease. Such were the catalysis for hope lost. We prayed to God that we

would die soon and quickly. For many of my fellow knight prisoners, God answered their prayers.

I was not so fortunate. My maddening anguish endured, and abysmal despair enveloped me. I resigned my soul to God, but the tortuous days passed without relief—each more oppressing than the previous. In the loudest voice I could muster, I pleaded with God to take me to Him, "For what sins am I to suffer so? I am a righteous man who has scrupulously followed your commandments and the laws of the Church. In your name, I fought the Muslims in Palestine and Syria. My blood is on Holy soil." For divine reasons, He did not answer my prayers. My only consolation was that He had other plans for me to serve him.

Much later, I learned that Saladin had ordered humane treatment for Christian prisoners. Reports noted that he was kind, empathetic, and obliging. He was a devout Muslim and followed all its tenets scrupulously, including those concerning the treatment of non-believers. Disregarding his orders, his soldiers only took knights as prisoners. They murdered our squires and regular soldiers on the spot of their capture. Clearly, our jailers ignored his instructions, regarding the treatment of prisoners.

One morning, I do not know its calendar day or year; the warden opened my cell door and ordered me to follow him. Weakly I arose and stumbled after him. What had I done I wondered? Is it to be another flogging? Too numb to understand and too fearful to ask, I stumbled after the jailer. Shortly, we arrived at the main gate.

"What is happening?" I whispered in what voice I could muster. There was no response. Guards unlocked the gate and swung it open, and with a flourish, the warden pushed me outside. The bright sun blinded me, and without strength of body or will, I collapsed to the ground.

Shortly, a well-manicured hand grabbed my left arm and pulled me up upright. I saw a tall young man dressed in fine flowing robe and a bejeweled turban. Overwhelming his countenance was a look of indignant disgust at the wretch of a human he was holding steady—a Christian knight infested with vermin, filthy, fetid, emaciated, and in tatters. Quickly he regained his equanimity, "I am Prince Yusuf al Khaleel, third cousin of Saladin, the Sultan of Egypt and Syria. Saladin has sent me to escort you to Hebron."

Unable to understand, I muttered several unintelligible sounds, "Why to such a place? Am I to be imprisoned there?" The prince did not respond. Two of his lackeys placed me in a plush carriage pulled by two white stallions. We

rode in the blazing desert, for how long I do not know. Eventually, we entered a lush oasis. Near the large central pool, which was surrounded by palm trees and lush grass, I spotted a large white tent. Atop its center pole was the ensign of Saladin fluttering in the light breeze—a bright green flag with a black crescent and star, and the Arabic words for "Praise Allah."

Thick Persian carpets covered the sand floor, and multi-colored drapes hung from the ceiling. Seven young women surrounded me and stripped me naked. I was too weak to protest or to be embarrassed. One gasped at my scars as she offered fresh, cool water. I drank deeply. Another woman offered me a tray of figs and dates. I stared blankly at the tray. She carefully placed a date in my mouth. Never had I tasted a food so sweet. Then I ate a fig. The woman refused me more saying, "Slowly, Christian knight, you must accustom your body to this rich diet."

Another indicated that I was to sit on a red silk divan. She shaved my beard, hair, and all parts of my body, and wiped me with a foul smelling solution. Later, two others indicated that I was to step into a deep bath of warm water that caressed my weary and bruised body. They scrubbed me with aromatic soaps and soft cloths. They refilled the bath time and time again until the water finally ran clear. Somewhat revived in mind and body, and luxuriating in sensual pleasures, I wondered if I was in Arcadia? Had God taken me while I was asleep? Reality surfaced as I felt the women vigorously drying me with white towels. Later, they massaged me with fragrant oils. One very young girl brought another container of water and offered a tray of sliced fruit: oranges, apricots, olives, avocados, and almonds. Incredulous at the cornucopia of delicacies I had not seen in years, I sampled one portion each.

Next, they dressed me in comfortable robes, escorted me to a large blue silk divan, and indicated that I was to lie down. Quite suddenly, I was exhausted and wobbled. Had I been drugged? I fell into the divan and sank into its folds. I felt a cool breeze. Forcing my eyes open, I saw two of the women slowly waving large fans over me. This is the last I remember of that day.

Sometime later, when I awoke, my hosts offered me roast goat and fish, onions, salt, bread, and honey, and fruit with smells so sweet. Baths and grooming followed. Towards evening, a very young woman escorted me outside the tent and led me in a short walk around the pool.

Without explanation, this was my treatment for many weeks. To avoid boredom and to keep my mind keen, they offered me books written in Latin

and Arabic—topics encompassed history, astronomy, agriculture, warfare, mathematics, and other subjects. With the continued healthy diet and longer and longer walks, my physical and mental strength improved daily. However, I was keenly troubled: why had I been chosen of all the knight prisoners for such lavish treatment? No matter my questions, the women would not or could not tell me why I was being treated so generously. What was the underlying purpose? Perhaps they did not know. Nor would they tell me the year, month, or day.

I do not know how many days had passed since my release. The days slipped away, one after another. Eventually, Prince Khaleel arrived. His look told me that he approved of my body's significant improvement. His words cracked, "Christian Knight Benito Cosimo, today I take you to Ashkelon. A boat under command of the Knights of St. John will arrive shortly to take you to Malta and then to your infidel country."

Completely mystified and yet overjoyed, I shouted, "I am free. 'Glory to God!'" Continuing in full voice I asked, "Why was I released from prison? Why am I being sent to Italy?"

With a scowl Prince Khaleel snapped, "You are indeed fortunate, Christian knight. You are one of the few to leave our Muslim land alive. In this year of 1193, your Pope has paid a ransom of five thousand gold coins to Saladin for you, and with the condition that we return you to Italy in good health in body and mind. It has been arranged."

What a staggering revelation. I was dumbfounded. Could it be that I was in that Saracen prison for only three years? More important, for what reason would the Pope want me? I did not know the Pope, and I had no connections with any of his synod. In fact, I did not know if Clement was still the reigning Pope.

Two

My journey to Naples was uneventful. On debarking, a delegation from the Vatican met me and immediately escorted me to Rome. To my persistent question, "Why?" no one in my retinue would respond. In fact they did not say much of anything. Two days later, we entered the Vatican and Papal Guards escorted us to the Apostolic Palace. On entering, a red-clad cardinal took my hand and said, "I am Cardinal Alfonzo Loren DeLuca, the Prefect of the Congregation for the Doctrine of Faith, "Welcome home Sir Giovanni Benito Cosimo. Your voyage was satisfactory?"

Before I could respond, he started walking and continued, "I am to take you to meet his Holiness Pope Celestine III. Follow me."

Now I was more confused than ever. What had I done to have an audience with this Pope? Who is he? As we approached the Pope's office, two guards swung open the large gold-plated doors. "Send that brave knight to me," commanded the Pope.

I approached him cautiously, scarcely daring to look at him. I knelt at his feet and kissed the Ring of the Fisherman on the third finger of his right hand.

He gestured for me to sit in a chair to the side of his desk. Standing on his right was another cardinal. The Pope nodded toward him. "Sir Cosimo, this is my Secretary of State, Cardinal Francesco Lombardi Rizzo."

Stunned at this august assemblage gathered to see me, I was without voice. In recognition, I nodded to the cardinal.

The Pope continued, "Sir Cosimo, we are delighted to see you safe and well in Christendom."

He saw my confusion and in a soft voice said, "I will answer you questions shortly."

I nodded in understanding.

"I have ransomed you because I have a sacred commission for you— one of great importance. As I understand, you have no family; accordingly, you will live in the Vatican. First, I want you to rest and gather your thoughts. Then you will write all the details of your adventures in the Holy Land and give them to Cardinal Rizzo. We are most interested in the inner workings of Saladin's Muslim empire. I am confident that you have much to contribute. I will call for you in a few days. Recall the names and nationalities of all the knights imprisoned with you—those deceased and those remaining." He stood to signal that the interview was over. I bowed again and Cardinal DeLuca escorted me out of the room

✦ ✦ ✦

On Sunday afternoon I was again with the Pope and his two cardinals. "Sir Cosimo, join me in savoring one of my vineyards' finest red wines. Relax, and let us enjoy the moment."

"Your Holiness, I am honored to share your wine."

Several minutes passed. At last I could no longer remain silent, "Pray tell, why you have paid such an exorbitant ransom for me? I have no family connections with the Church. I have no land, no fortune, nor much of anything to serve you. I am an itinerant knight in search of a commission."

"You underestimate yourself, Sir Cosimo. You have rare gifts that distinguish you from many others in Christendom. I have read your report with utmost interest, and its details confirm the facts in your file. You have mastered several of the Muslim languages; you know their customs; you are tested in battle and survived the most horrid imprisonment. Yes, you will do well for me."

"Please excuse me your Holiness. You mentioned facts in my file. I am at a loss to understand how the Vatican could assemble a file on me without knowing anything about me."

"My answer is simple and confidential. Do you swear to secrecy?"

"Yes of course, your Holiness."

Cardinal DeLuca, who had been walking behind me, moved to my side, "The Vatican has informants throughout the known world."

Before I could respond, the Pope intervened "Let us turn to the business at hand. Your commission is to find the Patriarch Prester John and to deliver my pastoral letter to him. I have commanded him and his Nestorian Christian nation to submit to the authority of the Pope of Rome as the Magisterium of all Christendom and the direct successor of Saint Peter. To entice him to accept, I have offered two promises: with slight modification to his faith, he may have a Nestorian church in Rome, and have an altar in the Church of the Holy Sepulcher in Jerusalem."

Cardinal DeLuca continued, "Take the Pope's letter enclosed in this leather pouch and sealed with the ring of St. Peter. We are not sure where his Christian nation is located. At best, we estimate it is somewhere in the Orient—perhaps in India. In fact, we are chagrined to admit that we do not know whether Prester John and his Nestorian kingdom are real. Rumors and apocryphal information about him abound with enough intensity and frequency that we must investigate."

The cardinal turned to the Pope seeming to ask if he should proceed. At an unseen signal, he continued, "Nonetheless, Prester John is critically important to our European Christian civilization for three reasons. He practices an unorthodox Christian faith that must be modified to conform to the tenets of the Nicene Creed of Rome, and he and his flock must submit to the Pope's authority as the spiritual and temporal leader of Christendom. Lastly, his immense wealth could finance additional crusades that would free the Holy Land from the Saracens for all time.

With trepidation, I accepted the letter pouch, "I will do my best, Your Holiness. However, I am at a loss about how I am to travel safely in Muslim lands. Surely I will be captured, and killed and your letter destroyed."

Cardinal Lombardi interceded, "A clause in your ransom contract demands that you have safe passage and unwavering support in your travels. We have a warrant signed by Saladin that allows you and your accompanying escort unlimited and protected passage through all Muslim lands. Also, he has agreed to publish this warrant throughout his domain."

Totally overwhelmed but with firm conviction I responded, "I understand, Your Eminence."

The cardinal continued, "Before you depart, I shall ensure that you are well-funded in gold coins and have a copy of our contract with Saladin. We

have assembled an escort for you of ten knights and their squires, and three scribes to record your travels. Lastly, from time to time send me a report of your progress."

"Godspeed, Sir Cosimo," the Pope said as he gave me his papal blessing.

Three

Prior to my departure for the Orient, I visited the Papal library to research the dossier on Prester John. The Pope gave me unlimited authority to search all relevant documents. My summary findings reveal that Prester John is the chimerical king of a royal domain of Nestorian Christians who are lost amidst the Muslims and pagans in the Orient. He is a "Presbyter" because he is highly successful at converting pagans and those of other faiths to his interpretation of Christianity. Some records describe his kingdom as located in India. In others, the Nestorians are centered in Persia, or perhaps they are in the Caucasus of Central Asia. Portuguese explorers reported that his kingdom is in Africa, somewhere in the highlands of Christian Ethiopia.

Some ecclesiastics averred that Prester John is a fantasy. Others decried him as a heretic. Still others charged him as a charlatan. No one in Christendom knows for sure. Nonetheless, there are numerous reports from Christian missionaries and explorers, and from Muslim records that he exists. In one of the library's large secret folders on Prester John, I found letters supposedly written by him and sent to the last three popes. They are written in a language I cannot read, and there is no deciphered text in the folders. Are such letters forgeries? These letters could be authenticated only with direct testimony from Prester John written in Latin and certified by credible witnesses.

Myths about Patriarch Prester John's kingdom abound, and their veracity range from possible to absurd. The myth possibly started in the third century with the stories of St. Thomas in his Acts of Thomas and his telling of a fabulous kingdom in the East. Or, perhaps Prester John was the early Christian figure John the Presbyter of Syria of the late first

century. Alternately, he is described as a lineal descendent of Ogier the Dane who penetrated into the north of India in the third century. In some documents, he is a descendant of one of the Three Magi that attended the infant Jesus Christ. How old must he be? I wonder.

I found a hastily scribbled marginally note on a letter from Pope Alexander III to the bishop of Naples, dated March 1, 1160. The note tells of the Archbishop of India's visit to Rome for an audience with the Pope to discuss Prester John and his Nestorian Christians. There was nothing else. I could not authenticate this note.

According to legend, Prester John's kingdom is fabulously wealthy. It abounds in treasures from the Orient: gold, emeralds, and all manner of precious gems, silk, ivory, rare incenses, spices, and salt. Within his kingdom are the Gates of Alexander, the Fountain of Youth; and the Phoenix lives there. He has a magical mirror in which he can see all provinces of his realm. And his kingdom borders Avalon, the Earthly Paradise. Do Prester John and his kingdom exist? No one can answer this question with certainty.

A few days later, my company and I set sail for Rhodes.

Four

It was late in 1193 when we arrived in Acre. Prince Yusuf al Khaleel met us at the dock. With him was a squadron of Saracen soldiers. With obvious disdain, Khaleel looked carefully at every person in my company, and finally said, "I represent Pasha Sidi ben Aidi, the governor of this Muslim province of Syria. My duty, Christian knight, is to guarantee your safe passage to Baghdad. Beyond, you may travel freely without escort anywhere in our Muslim land." On his command, the Saracens surrounded us. Their sullen expressions and obvious distaste for their task were ominous.

Fearing that we were betrayed, I shouted, "Is this your guarantee of safe passage?" I would not be a Muslim prisoner again. "Knights, draw your swords and defend yourself."

With a commanding voice the Prince responded, "Stop, Christian knight. Order your men to drop their weapons. Do it now! I guarantee your safety only if you disarm."

Startled at this outrageous command, I snapped, "By whose order are we to disarm?"

"Mine," he snapped. "Either disarm or return to Rhodes. There is no other option."

Realizing that we had no choice and with trepidation, I ordered my men to lay down their arms and to do nothing that would provoke our escort.

His Saracens gathered our weapons and stored them in a horse-drawn, two-wheeled cart.

"A wise choice, Christian knight. Your weapons will be returned when you leave Muslim lands."

As we were about to leave the dock area, the Prince said, "I caution you and all in your company not to display a cross, mention Christendom, or

to practice any aspect of your faith." He paused for effect. "Any such display would be singularly offensive and would negate my guarantee of your safety."

As abhorrent as are the prince's admonitions, I spoke to my company, "Fellow knights, obey the prince's commands. If we are to succeed, we must scrupulously adhere to the customs of our host in this Muslim land. We dare not offend."

Having agreed to his mandates, the prince ordered, "Have your men mount their horses and follow me. My soldiers will follow in trail." On his command, the entourage trotted into the center of the city. We stopped at a large white tent with large green banners billowing from the support poles with inscriptions that read in Arabic, "God Is Great."

"Here is your shelter for the night. Inside there is food and water. We leave at sunrise tomorrow."

The next day we started our journey to Baghdad. The prince spoke to me only when necessary. Two weeks later we reached the Gate of Syria, the western entrance to Baghdad—the Nizari Caliphate of Islam. The prince led us to the entrance of the Golden Gate Palace. "You will stay here for a few days to work with our geographers and scholars to help plan your travels into Persia and India. And, it has been arranged for you to have an audience with our Imam-Caliph, Muizz A'lā Muhammed—a unique privilege for a Christian. Sit on the stool offered and say nothing. The Imam-Caliph knows you understand Arabic. Nod at appropriate times. At length, he will dismiss you with a wave of his right hand. Arise, and walk backward out of his chamber. No matter the circumstance, do not turn your back to the Imam-Caliph. Such an insult will cause your beheading.

My audience with the Imam-Caliph lasted but a few minutes and was of no significance. He told me how great he is as the leader of the Muslim world, averred that Mohammed is the true prophet, and asked if I would convert to Mohammedanism. Without waiting for an answer, he waved his right hand and his retainers escorted me out of the palace.

Within a week, my troop and I left Baghdad and began our journey to find Prester John and his kingdom. We spent six years exploring Mesopotamia. We investigated the sites that the Muslim geographers suggested. We also explored the ancient cities of Ur, Nineveh, Babylon, and Samarra. We searched a host of other sites following clues that seemed plausible. We found no evidence that Prester John or his king-

dom existed in Mesopotamia. Over these six years, I sent three knights back to Rome to report on our activities and our failure to find this apocryphal king.

We spent the next seven years exploring Persia. We visited the ancient cities of Persepolis, Shushan, Hamadan, Ardabil, and dozens more. Several of my knights fell ill to a mysterious fever and expired. There was no evidence of Prester John in Persia.

We ventured north into the Caucasus—spending three years exploring all possible sightings and clues. We failed to uncover any trace of Prester John.

The two knights left of my escort and I spent the next six years exploring India: the foothills of the Himalayas in Sikkim, the deserts of Baluchistan, the glaciers of Kashmir, the high plains of the Punjab, the river valleys of Assam, and the jungles of Tamil Nadu. Again, there was no evidence of Prester John or his Kingdom. To my dismay, my remaining two knights died in this place: one from a poisonous serpent strike, and the other due to fever.

In my sixth year in India, I had an audience with the Nizam of Hyderabad. He said that had he heard of Prester John, but he did not know where his kingdom is. He continued, "I have hearsay from traveling Portuguese merchants that he resides in the high mountains of central Africa in the Kingdom of Ethiopia."

✦ ✦ ✦

For twenty-two years, I searched assiduously for Prester John without success. I explored the Orient: Mesopotamia, Persia, the Caucasus, and India: explored the unexplored, and places not named. I traveled the Silk Road and its ancillary routes. I quizzed moguls, princes, camel herders, priests, imams, merchant traders, travelers of all nationalities, faiths, and races for information about Prester John. None gave accurate intelligence. Some admitted no knowledge of him, a few gave precise directions that proved to be erroneous, and others had second and third-hand information about him but did not know his location. Others made wild speculations where his kingdom is located: it is a short distance over the next mountain range; perhaps it is over the next roaring river, or it is far away across that desert just over the horizon.

I searched all these rumored locations and other sites that I figured were a reasonable possibility. I found no evidence of Prester John or his kingdom.

Now, I was alone. I was physically exhausted and mentally weary. I wondered if I had the will or the stamina to continue this futile search. On reflection, I was obligated to continue to obey faithfully my Pope's charge to deliver his pastoral letter to Prester John. Perhaps the Portuguese explorers were correct: his kingdom is in Ethiopia.

Five

I departed India from the port of Goa on a five-masted Chinese junk bound for the Arabian coast. The captain's port of call was Ubar, the hub of the frankincense route. It took ten days to navigate the Arabian Sea sailing against a westerly wind. After three days of trading in Ubar, the captain set sail for Adulis—Ethiopia's primary port. After sailing for another three days in the Gulf of Aden, the captain turned north into the Red Sea. Two days later, I disembarked the junk in Adulis.

Without a plan or resources, I wandered about the city for a while until I spotted a Christian church. Inside I found a Coptic priest, introduced myself, and told him of my Papal writ to find King Prester John and his Christian Nestorian Kingdom.

"Welcome to Ethiopia, Sir Cosimo." I have heard of this mythical king but have no credible knowledge of him. Our king, Gebre Mesqel, has the honorific title of 'Prester John.' However, he is not the king you seek. Our king awarded this title to himself as the founder of the Solomonic Dynasty in Ethiopia and the leader of our Coptic religion. His interest was piqued by Portuguese traders' accounts of Prester John and his fabulous kingdom which they say is located here in Africa."

Intrigued by this information and with a surge of renewed purpose, I commented, "Indeed, I need to meet your king to enlist his support in my search for Prester John. Will you help me arrange such a meeting? I am at my wits' end. I have no clues where to search, no resources, and I do not have the mental or physical strength to explore Ethiopia without help and expert guidance."

"Indeed, your search is at a critical juncture. Tomorrow, I will send an acolyte to the Holy City of Lalibela with my letter to our king to in-

troduce you and to explain your mission. I estimate it will be four to six weeks for a response. Meantime, I offer you haven in my monastery—time for you to revitalize."

✦ ✦ ✦

One morning, about six weeks later, I was in the monastery's garden updating this journal recording my exploration of India. My health and vigor had returned to near normal for a man of forty seven years. I was immersed in writing when a soft, melodious voice spoke, "Good day, sir. Are you Knight Cosimo?"

Startled, I looked up and saw the most beautiful woman I had ever seen. I stumbled in my response, "Yes, I am Giovanni Benito Cosimo."

Smiling, she continued. "I am Sarah, King Mesqel's, youngest daughter. My father has sent me to guide you to the Holy City of Lalibela and his home."

She was perhaps nineteen or twenty. Her long, jet-black hair was tied in intricate knots, her purple-black skin shone to a fine luster; her features were those of the classical Aphrodite. She moved with a subtle grace. Recovering from my astonishment, I said, "That is most kind of you and your father. I am eager to meet him and discuss my search for Prester John. I need to assemble my belongings then I'll be ready to go."

"After my escorts refreshes themselves and tend to their horses, we can leave. I have brought a horse for you. Our journey to Lalibela will be four days. I am sure my father will pleased to hear about your journeys and to discuss your efforts to find Prester John."

"I shall tell him all that I know and will enlist his aid to help me explore your country. Ethiopia is the last area that I have information as to the location of this ephemeral king."

I thanked my host for his hospitality, and mounted the horse. Then Sarah, her twelve soldiers, and I trotted away, heading for highland valleys in the mountains. One morning on the third day, we stopped at a stream to refresh ourselves. As I approached the stream, I stepped on what I thought was a small tree branch. It was a serpent. It struck me in the right calf. The pain was intense and I fell to the ground in agonizing pain, and wondered if this was the end of my journey.

Seeing what happened, Sarah ran to me, drew her knife, and dug deep into the fang marks and sucked out the bloody poison. I fainted. Later that evening I awoke, and it felt as if my whole body was on fire. My leg had swollen to twice its normal size and Sarah had applied bandages over the wounds.

"Sir Cosimo, you indeed are fortunate to have survived. You were bitten by a mamba, one of the most deadly and aggressive serpents in all Africa. Few survive its bite. We will rest here for a few days for you to recover."

"I owe you my life, Sarah. I am in your debt and shall try to repay you in some way."

"Please, Sir Cosimo, it is not necessary. We are pleased to have you as our guest."

✦ ✦ ✦

At Lalibela, Sarah introduced me to her father, King Gebre Mesqel. He was a tall, handsome fellow, and a gracious host. He welcomed me enthusiastically, "I am honored to have you, a Christian knight, an emissary of the Pope in Rome, as my guest. Please consider my home as yours."

For several days, I told him of my searches for Prester John. The king questioned me closely, asking for specific details. "What clues did you have? What sites did you visit and what did you find there? What princes did you meet? With whom did you talk?" He followed with a myriad of other questions probing deeply into what I had discovered.

"I concluded my tale with, "I have explored the Orient for twenty-two years to find this King and without success. I have investigated all clues, hints, and myths about his location, all to no avail. My last area to survey is your beautiful country, Ethiopia."

Satisfied that he had extracted all the pertinent information I had, he asked, "In all your journeys, have you any real evidence that Prester John exists?"

"None."

Reflecting on my accounts, he began to tell me about his efforts to find this ephemeral Prester John. "I have sent several expeditions seeking him. My agents have explored throughout Ethiopia—along our great river, our lakes, and in the high plains. They have ventured into the Muslim

north, and scoured central Africa to the Indian Ocean. All have returned without success. Now, I am convinced that Prester John, if he exists, is not in Africa."

Startled at this announcement, I paused to reflect on its impact on my holy writ. "At the moment, I am surprised at your analysis because central Africa was the last place left for me to find this Nestorian Kingdom. Yet, I am relieved by your conclusion. In all probability, my search is over. Nonetheless, with your permission, I want to incorporate in my journal the accounts of your expeditions' failures to find Prester John, and to conclude, that King Prester John and his kingdom are apocryphal."

"Please do, Sir Cosimo. It is best to end this fairy tale once and for all."

I spent the next few months in Lalibela, luxuriating in a semi-paradise—talking with the king, exploring the countryside with Sarah, trying to make myself useful, and to be a gracious guest. From time to time, I worked on plans for my return to Rome—a difficult task because I had no resources and no support. The last correspondence I sent to the Pope was when I departed Goa. Troubling me is that I've had no indication that any of my messages had reached the Pope or that he was still interested in my mission.

One evening at dinner, somewhat chagrinned, I discussed my problem with the king and asked for his support.

"Of course I will help you return to Rome and deliver your important journal." He paused and smilingly looked at Sarah, then turned to me. "Sarah speaks well and often of you. I suspect that she is smitten with you."

Flushed with embarrassment and not knowing exactly how to respond, I replied, "I am flattered that your charming daughter would find me, an old man, of some romantic interest." I smiled at Sarah and turned to look at her father, "I must confess that I find your daughter attractive. And I shall be reluctant and saddened to leave this nonpareil realm, your gracious hospitality, and the lovely Sarah."

The king clapped his hands loudly and let out a loud guffaw. "Then it is done." He stood, grabbed Sarah's hand and placed it on my heart. "I offer you Sarah, my youngest daughter, for your bride."

"Without reflection, I blurted, "Thank you Sire. I am honored to have Sarah as my wife. And with your permission we will make our life here in the highlands of Ethiopia."

A few days later, a Coptic priest performed the marriage ceremony. At the wedding reception, the King offered me a house on the River Jordan close by his home.

✦ ✦ ✦

Three years and two sons later, I have a home and a family. For the first time in all my years, I am enjoying life and I am content, peaceful, and fulfilled. Although I have a lingering pang of guilt for abandoning my mission without the Pope's permission, I rationalized that I've done all I am able to do. My mission to find Prester John and his Nestorian kingdom was a fool's errand.

Unannounced, one day the Holy Knight George Maxwell Chamberlain in the service of Pope Honorius III, and his entourage arrive in Lalibela. After a curt introduction, the knight snapped, "Pope Honorius is disappointed that you have not sent him a report of your search for Prester John for several years. He wonders if you have abandoned your quest for this renegade Christian?"

With complete calm, I rejoined, "The Pope is correct. I have abandoned my quest for Prester John. He does not exist, and I say that unequivocally. The Pope will have to continue his crusades without that mythical king's supposed fabulous wealth."

"Knight, Sir Cosimo, the Pope has charged me to deliver his Holy Writ that commands you to continue your search for Prester John and to send frequent reports to him."

"I repeat, there is no Prester John, and his kingdom of Nestorian Christians does not exist. He is a fable, a myth, a fairy tale. There is no point in continuing to look for a phantom."

"You are wrong Sir Cosimo. We have new intelligence on Prester John's location. A defrocked priest has knelt before the Pope, pleaded for forgiveness for his hearsay, and offered presents from Prester John and a letter in Latin asking for an audience. The best this priest could tell is that Prester John's kingdom is located somewhere in the high mountains to the north of India, perhaps in China. The priest could not be more specific."

"Is this letter authentic?, I asked dubiously. "How did the priest get this letter? Has it been verified? Is it a forgery?"

"Pope Honorius believes the letter to be authentic. To confirm his sincerity, Prester John sent the Pope a solid gold cross. Its horizontal bar is a long as a man's forearm. And it is encrusted with precious jewels: rubies, emeralds, jade, lapis lazuli, sapphires, and stones that we cannot identify."

"Sir Chamberlain, your report is most interesting. Regrettably, I cannot comply with the Pope's writ. I am too old, and I do not have the mental energy or the physical stamina to conduct another extensive search for Prester John. Now, I live here in Ethiopia. I have a home, a dutiful wife, and two beautiful children. I am content to live here in this Coptic Christian country to love my beautiful wife, play with my boys, and guide them to grow into honorable men.

"Sir Cosimo, you are impertinent. I speak with the authority of our new Pope, Honorius III. You are compelled to comply with the papal holy writ which endures no matter who is our current Pope."

"I understand. Nonetheless, I respectfully decline to continue my search. In this Coptic Christian mountain kingdom, Pope Honorius has no authority. I have devoted twenty-two years searching with all my ability to find Prester John and deliver Pope Celestine's holy writ to him. I failed, and I am unable to do more. Please send my deepest regrets to Pope Honorius and return to him Pope Celestine's letter to Prester John. To complete my service to the Holy See, deliver this journal of my travels these past twenty-five years—three of these years in a Muslim prison.

"Sir Giovanni Benito Cosimo, you must realize that your defiance of a holy writ is grounds for excommunication."

"Yes, that is the procedure." I looked away for a moment of reflection. I realized that God's mercy extends beyond the real of the Pope of Rome. And I am content with the life I have found in the highlands of Ethiopia. With a deep sense of finality, I said, "I will have an escort take you and your entourage to Khartoum on the upper Nile. From there you can sail to Alexandria. Have a safe journey."

FIN

Other fiction by S. Martin Shelton
www.sheltoncomm.com

St. Catherine's Crown

Aviators, Adventurers, & Assassins

Abyssinia

Ming Yellow